"I am sorry that I attempted to trap you with a kiss," Gino said.

"Not in the plan, for sure," Roz blurted out. Her insides went tight as Gino stepped closer.

"Who is Louise Odier? You have her name written down on this paper."

"Omigosh, she's a rose."

Gino picked up the paper and read out with lead weights of emphasis, "'Ask Rowie about Louise Odier!!!' Three exclamation points, Dr. Madison. And you are an acknowledged expert on roses." He stepped closer. "If you wrote this, who is Rowie? Or possibly it's better to ask, 'Who are *you?*' Because despite the uncanny resemblance, the woman who kissed me back with such heat just now—" his gaze dropped to her lips, which suddenly felt soft and wouldn't stay pressed together "—is quite definitely *not* the one who outlined her plans for my garden in a meeting several weeks ago, is she?"

Dear Reader,

Just as the seasons change, you may have noticed that our Silhouette Romance covers have evolved over the past year. We have tried to create cover art that uses more soft pastels, sun-drenched images and tender scenes to evoke the aspirational and romantic spirit of this line. We have also tried to make our heroines look like women you can relate to and may want to be. After all, this line is about the joys of falling in love, and we hope you can live vicariously through these heroines.

Our writers this month have done an especially fine job in conveying this message. Reader favorite Cara Colter leads the month with *That Old Feeling* (#1814) in which the heroine must overcome past hurts to help her first love raise his motherless daughter. This is the debut title in the author's emotional new trilogy, A FATHER'S WISH. Teresa Southwick concludes her BUY-A-GUY miniseries with the story of a feisty lawyer who finds herself saddled with an unwanted and wholly irresistible bodyguard, in *Something's Gotta Give* (#1815). A sister who'd do anything for her loved ones finds her own sweet reward when she switches places with her sibling, in *Sister Swap* (#1816)— a compelling new romance by Lilian Darcy. Finally, in *Made-To-Order Wife* (#1817) by Judith McWilliams, a billionaire hires an etiquette expert to help him land the perfect society wife, and he soon starts rethinking his marriage plans.

Be sure to return next month when Cara Colter continues her trilogy and Judy Christenberry returns to the line.

Happy reading!

Ann Leslie Tuttle
Associate Senior Editor

Please address questions and book requests to:
Silhouette Reader Service
U.S.: 3010 Walden Ave., P.O. Box 1325, Buffalo, NY 14269
Canadian: P.O. Box 609, Fort Erie, Ont. L2A 5X3

LILIAN DARCY

SISTER SWAP

SILHOUETTE *Romance*®

Published by Silhouette Books

America's Publisher of Contemporary Romance

SILHOUETTE BOOKS

ISBN 0-373-19816-7

SISTER SWAP

Visit Silhouette Books at www.eHarlequin.com

Printed in U.S.A.

Books by Lilian Darcy

Silhouette Romance

The Baby Bond #1390
Her Sister's Child #1449
Raising Baby Jane #1478
*Cinderella After Midnight #1542
*Saving Cinderella #1555
*Finding Her Prince #1567
Pregnant and Protected #1603
For the Taking #1620
The Boss's Baby Surprise #1729
The Millionaire's Cinderella Wife #1772
Sister Swap #1816

Silhouette Special Edition

Balancing Act #1552
Their Baby Miracle #1672
The Father Factor #1696

*The Cinderella Conspiracy

LILIAN DARCY

has written over fifty books for Silhouette Romance, Special Edition and Harlequin Mills & Boon Medical Romance (Prescription Romance). Her first book for Silhouette appeared on the Waldenbooks Series Romance bestsellers list, and she's hoping readers go on responding strongly to her work. Happily married with four active children and a very patient cat, she enjoys keeping busy and could probably fill several more lifetimes with the things she likes to do—including cooking, gardening, quilting, drawing and traveling. She currently lives in Australia but travels to the United States as often as possible to visit family. Lilian loves to hear from readers. You can write to her at P.O. Box 381, Hackensack NJ 07602 or e-mail her at lildarcy@austarmetro.com.au.

Dear Reader,

Although I don't know anywhere near as much about roses as my heroine's sister, I do consider them to be the most fascinating and beautiful of flowers. My love for them was first kindled when we lived in Columbus, Ohio, within walking distance of the gorgeous Whetstone Park of Roses.

I had toddlers and babies then, and I used to take the stroller and wander around the gardens in all seasons, but particularly when the roses were in bloom…and so were the brides. Many couples chose to exchange their vows in such a lovely setting, and because I'm such a die-hard romantic I loved going to the Park of Roses on a Saturday afternoon and peeking at the bride and her attendants from a discreet distance. I would admire their gowns against the backdrop of pink and yellow and red roses in full bloom, and point them out to my children as I unstrapped them from the stroller so they could play on the grass. "See the beautiful bride?" Happily married myself, I always gave a silent wish that these brides and grooms would be just as lucky.

Sister Swap has this same feeling, I hope. Romance and roses, happiness and hope, set against the backdrop of a beautiful garden, with children playing on the grass.

Happy reading.

Lilian Darcy

Chapter One

"So, Mom, she's been stuck in that hotel room for two days, until you could get there," Roxanna said, "because she's been too scared to leave it on her own?"

"This is going to ruin her career, Rox!" Roxanna's mother answered, over the phone. She was calling from London, a hotel near Heathrow Airport, but she sounded clear enough to be in the next building—and clear enough that every bit of her distress came through.

"Mom, it's going to ruin her life! She needs treatment. This is a major anxiety disorder, and it's getting worse. She has to see that."

"You have to fly to Italy and cover for her at the Di Bartoli family estate. This is a big project, and she needs it on her résumé. She can't have it turn into a disaster, after all the work and study she's done."

"Oh, right! Cover for her, because I know everything

there is to know about antique roses and historic garden restoration? You can't be serious!"

Rox knew almost nothing about the subject, as Mom was well aware. She was a singer…well, a waitress with a music teaching degree she'd never used, but she didn't want to examine that issue right now.

"Cover for her, because I'm one of the few people in the world who can tell the two of you apart," Mom said.

"I weigh eight pounds more than she does, and I have way stronger lungs."

"Nobody notices that. Especially if they don't even know that Rowena has an identical twin sister."

"True. She hasn't mentioned my existence to the Di Bartoli family?"

"No, she says she definitely hasn't. Honey, Rowie has promised that if you do this for her, she will get treatment. Yes, even she can see how much she needs it now."

Rox closed her eyes, seeking inner guidance.

How could she say no? As Mom had just reminded her, she and Rowena were identical twins. Their bond was deep and life-long and complex, and it was important to both of them. They'd developed in such different ways, thanks to Rowena's much greater frailty at birth and beyond, but the bond hadn't lessened or changed.

Rowena, in particular, tugged on it a lot. This wouldn't be the first time Roxanna had bailed her out when she'd been seized by one of her increasingly severe and increasingly frequent attacks of paralyzing anxiety. The one difference was that this time, thank heavens, Row had conceded she needed professional help.

Okay, there were a couple of other differences, too. Firstly, Rox had never been required to cross the

Atlantic Ocean to impersonate her sister before. Secondly, her schedule was…um…unusually light right now, so she couldn't plead a previous commitment.

She'd lost her job last Friday—her waitressing job— because her singing audition had run three hours late. Fortunately, this wasn't going to send her into major debt, because her expenses were currently low. She'd moved into her parents' house in northern New Jersey after her divorce late last year, taking care of it for them while they tried out a retirement move to Florida.

Footnote—she'd lost out at Friday's audition, hadn't even made the final cut, because the stress over the divorce was still affecting her voice.

Or maybe her voice just wasn't good enough.

That had been listed as Reason Number Seventeen on the twenty-one-item list her ex-husband Harlan had given her as to why it was her fault, not his, that he'd started an affair and left her. "Your voice isn't half as good as you think it is."

"So you'll fly Rowena back from London and find a therapist for her in Florida?" Rox asked her mother. There was no point in getting treatment for Rowie if they didn't do it right. "You'll take care of her until she's made some progress? You'll make sure she doesn't run away from the therapy?"

"That seems like the best plan. The only plan. It was all her mixed-up feelings about Francesco Di Bartoli that triggered this panic attack, but it's gone beyond anything rational, now. If she can't even leave the hotel room on her own, she can't possibly go back to Italy."

"So what has she told the Di Bartoli family about all this?"

"That she's been delayed in England, ordering the roses, but she should be back in Tuscany within a few days. Nothing about the underlying problem. So of course you'll have to fly to Rome via London, so Signor Di Bartoli isn't meeting you off a flight from the wrong continent."

"I can't pull this off, Mom. Surely Francesco will guess?"

"You can pull it off. You have to. He won't guess. He doesn't know you exist, and he hasn't known Rowena for that long. As an impersonation, being your sister is not that big a stretch for you. Rowena is on her laptop right now, collating her notes for you and printing out every detail you'll need, on top of all the books and notes still in Italy. And you can phone each other. You always left it till the last minute to cram for exams. This will be no different."

Mom was probably right.

Harlan had mentioned it, too. Reason Number Twelve. "You always leave everything till the last minute."

"Okay," she told her mother. "But only because she's promised to get treatment. I'll call the airlines and get on the first flight I can." Being someone who left things until the last minute, she was comfortable with traveling at short notice.

"Tonight?" Mom asked. It was currently Monday morning in New Jersey, Monday afternoon in Europe.

"I'll try."

"Call me back with the details. Then I can make plans for Rowie and me. We'll need to connect with you in London on your way through, so she can give you the information on the garden project."

Two days later, Roxanna touched down in Rome, wearing her twin sister's neat, professional clothes but feeling totally like herself inside. Scatty (Reason Number Five), imperfectly groomed (Number Fourteen) and, as previously discussed in Reason Twelve, ill-prepared.

"Pia, stay close to Papa," Gino said in Italian to his four-year-old daughter.

She strained at his hand, avid to explore the crowded airport terminal. He held her tighter, knowing only too well what would happen next, not having the slightest idea what to do about it.

I can't deal with one of her tantrums here.

Pia pulled harder, her face getting its stubborn look, her lungs building up a full head of steam, ready to start screaming and kicking and throwing her compact little body about. Miss Cassidy, Pia's English nanny, spent hours riding out the tantrums. She refused ever to give in, getting stricter and stricter the louder Pia screamed, until finally Pia would exhaust herself and fall asleep.

And I don't have the time for that, or the patience, Gino knew. *Lord help me, what is wrong with my child?*

How could a woman as perfect as Angele—serene, cool, competent in everything she did—have given birth to such a difficult little girl?

Abruptly, with his decision made before he even knew it, he released his grip on his daughter and watched her dart between the spring coats and business suits of those waiting to meet the London flight. Passengers had begun to appear. As long as Rowena Madison wasn't one of the last off the plane, he should be able to keep a rough eye on Pia's whereabouts and not lose her.

He'd only met Rowena a few times, but he was confident he'd recognize her right away. Based in Rome and with a senior executive role in the Di Bartoli family's multinational cosmetics corporation, he'd organized the initial interview with her regarding the garden restoration and had sat in on a couple of subsequent meetings to discuss her plans. The day-to-day liaison and supervision on the Di Bartoli estate itself he'd delegated to his thirty-three-year-old younger brother, Francesco.

Apparently Francesco had taken the liaison element way too seriously, however. Francesco had a perfectly charming and exceptionally suitable fiancée in Rome, and yet that hadn't stopped him from begging Rowena for an affair in Tuscany. According to Francesco, Rowena's trembling hesitation had only increased his desire.

Yes, well, so it would, Gino thought cynically. Francesco had always wanted something all the more when he found he couldn't get it too easily. He wasted large chunks of his life this way.

And Gino wasn't going to let him waste the prospect of a very good marriage on a stupid little affair with an American horticultural expert who didn't seem to know whether she wanted him or not, even if she was entitled to call herself Dr. Madison, thanks to her doctoral dissertation on seventeenth-century European garden design.

Where was Pia?

His heart thudded suddenly and he looked around in a panic. He couldn't see her. He should have dressed her in something brighter this morning. There weren't many bright outfits in her closet, however. As Angele had, Miss Cassidy favored exquisitely made French children's clothing in the same neutral colors—navy, gray and cream—that most of the adults in the airport were wearing. She was camouflaged as effectively as—

Ah. There she was. Safe. Intently watching a woman struggle with the jammed wheel of her suitcase.

And here was Rowena Madison.

She hadn't seen him yet. She was scanning faces with her eyes narrowed, and her teeth scraping across her lower lip, as if anxious that he might not have come. She wasn't to know how much he prided himself on his reliability.

He raised his hand and gestured, smiled and called her name. She saw him, and a strange series of expressions crossed her face, almost as if someone were trying out a series of different screen savers on a computer.

He had no idea what Francesco saw in her, despite how pretty she was with those deep blue eyes, the pale, creamy skin, the long dark hair loosely swept back. To Gino, she always seemed so prim and tame, like pasta cooked to mush instead of *al dente*—quite edible, yes, but not at all appetizing.

She pushed her way through the crowd toward him, a little breathless, with her wheeled and long-handled suitcase trundling behind her. She wore a neat beige pantsuit with a white silk blouse beneath. The blouse wasn't as neat as the suit. One of the middle buttons had come unfastened, showing the lower part of a white lacy bra and a shadowed stretch of the skin between her ribs. "Francesco…?" It wasn't quite a question.

"…couldn't come," Gino answered in his near-perfect English. He didn't apologize on his brother's behalf, since it wasn't his brother's fault.

He'd virtually ordered Francesco to stay in Rome to cool his head, while he himself took over the role of working with Rowena Madison on the garden. He could manage Di Bartoli business for a few weeks while based on the family's Tuscan estate, and he desperately wanted to get Pia out of Rome.

To see if that made a difference to the tantrums.

To find out how she behaved without the presence of the English nanny whom Angele had always praised to the skies.

To get to know his child.

"Francesco couldn't come," Rowena echoed. Her voice sounded a little throaty, deeper and richer than he remembered, as if it had gotten strained by the poor-quality air during the flight. Or maybe she had a cold.

"Sorry," he said, about Francesco's absence.

He wasn't sorry.

Was Dr. Madison? She did look a little shocked.

"Guess I'll just have to make do with you, then… uh…Gino." She threw him a dazzling, panicky grin.

The dazzle sent an odd jolt through him, and the panic made him curious. He'd already seen that she was somewhat an anxious, nervous type, but this seemed different. This wasn't a cage bunny's terror on being let out, but a wild hare's panic on being shut in.

But where was Pia?

Another, different kind of jolt. He'd lost Pia's mother, first through divorce and then through her untimely death. He wasn't going to lose his only child, as well.

This time, he really couldn't see her, and cursed her dove-gray dress again. Why not pink or bright lilac or something red with flowers? What sort of color was gray for a little girl?

"Is something wrong?" Roxanna asked Francesco's older brother.

Sheesh, she'd had a narrow escape on that one!

Never having seen either man before, she'd actually called him Francesco, but he'd thought she was talking *about* Francesco, asking why he wasn't here, so she'd gotten away with it. Then it had taken her three seconds too long to think of Gino's name. That was the problem with cramming for an exam the night before. Vital facts flew out of your head at the worst moments.

"Yes," he said, his dark eyes searching over Rox's shoulder. He was dressed for business in a charcoal suit, a white shirt and a conservative dark tie. As she watched, he reached for the tie knot and loosened it, which gave him a rakish, Cary Grant sort of look. Rox could tell he didn't even realize what he'd done. "I can't see my daughter. She's only four…"

And that was the problem with working from crib notes. Sometimes the vital facts just weren't there. She'd had no idea that Gino Di Bartoli had a daughter.

Did he have a wife?

And had Rowena met the daughter?

Because if Row has, then I should help look for her, because I'll supposedly know what she looks like. But I haven't met her, so how can I? What's her name?

"Pia!" Gino said, his voice rising. He spoke in Italian. "Pia, where are you?"

Whew! Again.

Pia, Pia, Pia. Remember that.

And luck was really running in Rox's favor today, because as soon as she saw the little girl in the pretty gray dress, she knew this had to be the one. She looked soooo like her daddy! She had fabulous, intelligent, dark hazel-brown eyes, a stubborn, perfectly shaped mouth, an equally stubborn jaw and lustrous ebony hair.

Rox pushed past several people to where Pia stood scribbling on a travel poster with a blue pen she'd probably found on the terminal floor. Gino had arrowed off in the opposite direction and didn't know yet that his daughter had been found, but Rox decided it would be better to actually collar Pia before alerting her papa. She looked like the kind of child who might disappear again at any moment.

"Pia, your papa is looking for you," she said in English. Did Pia speak English?

"I'm drawing," she said, which answered the question.

Roxanna spoke a bit of Italian, majored in it at college eight years ago when she had—no surprises, here—crammed for her Italian exams the night before. She hoped Pia's command of English was more extensive.

"Well, I think your papa would love to see your drawing," she said, "but then we have to get in the car and go, so let's stay right here until we see him."

"Very well," Pia said. Not *okay* Not even *all right*. Who the heck had taught her to say *very well?*

"Are you channeling Queen Victoria today, honey?" Rox murmured.

She grabbed a handful of Pia's full-skirted dress so that the child would be safely tethered in one spot without realizing it, and looked around for Signor Di Bartoli, whom she knew from Row's instructions she was supposed to call Gino.

Nice name.

Snappier than Francesco.

When she'd thought that he *was* Francesco, she'd had just enough time to decide it was no surprise that a man like this had triggered one of Rowie's major anxiety episodes. Even to Rox herself—and she never had anxiety attacks—he seemed a little scary. The kind of man who didn't put up with idiots or shirkers or cowards. The kind of man who demanded a lot from the people around him and got it. The kind of man who would kick Roxanna out of his palatial Tuscan estate the second he discovered she wasn't her twin sister, the garden expert.

She saw him over the tangle of arrivals. Couples kissed, businessmen shook hands, but Gino was still searching in the wrong direction. She waved and yoo-hooed.

Nope.

Then she put her voice into gear and practically sang, "Signor Di Bartoli! *Giii-nooo!*" Oh, those wonderful, operatic Italian names! It might be fun to brush up on her language skills while she was in Italy. "She's here. I've found her. We're over here."

A look of relief washed over his face like a tidal wave. It made Rox curious. Of course he cared about his little girl, but had he decided so fast that she was seriously lost?

Apparently, yes. When he reached her, he dropped low and gave her a huge hug, as if he hadn't seen her for weeks. But then he didn't really pay her drawing the proper attention, and that left Pia feeling way more lost than she'd felt while her papa was frantically looking for her.

Roxanna knew this because she knew how it felt when someone you cared about brushed your creativity aside. Harlan's Reason Number Sixteen—"You always expect me to make such a big ******* deal out of your singing." And she really could have done without the word he'd used between *big* and *deal*.

Uh-oh. What now?

Pia wanted to take the drawing with her. She'd already defaced a whole big corner of the travel poster. Actually removing it altogether would not look good for a thirty-five-year-old senior executive and principal shareholder in the renowned Di Bartoli Cosmetics Corporation.

"No, Pia," her papa said, speaking down at her from the impressive height he'd risen to after letting go of the hug. His face tightened. With anger?

No.

With dread.

Dread of the screaming that he could obviously see was going to start at any moment.

Rox could see it, too.

"Because, Pia," she said, quickly stepping close and bending down, "if we take it with us, everyone won't be able to see it anymore. All these people. Why don't we leave it here so it makes the airport prettier?"

She looked across the top of Pia's thick, satiny black hair, seeking Gino's approval. He looked startled. His mouth was shut hard—lips not too full, not too thin, she noticed. For a moment, she thought they were going to get the tantrum from him, instead. Then he gave a tight little nod.

"That's a very good idea, isn't it, Pia?" he said.

The little girl nodded and smiled and took the hand he held out. He looked relieved, and ready to flee the airport before something worse happened.

Another whew!

Lady Luck is soooo *blowing things my way today,* Rox thought. *Rowie would be happy with me, but it can't last.*

It didn't.

Walking toward the exit, Gino said, "You gave in to her." It was an accusation, not a compliment.

"Gave in to her?"

"But at least we avoided the tantrum."

Okay, so maybe that was kind of a compliment, but she couldn't let the *You gave in to her* bit go by.

Harlan's Reason Number Nine, incidentally. "You jump on every tiny thing."

"I didn't give in to her!" she said. "I made a positive suggestion that appealed to her, and deflected her feelings of frustration."

"We have been having serious problems with Pia's tantrums for a long time," Gino said, in a tone that could have frosted a pond. "We have a clear policy in place for dealing with them, and that involves never giving in to her. I appreciate that this time, in a very public locale, you managed to avoid the tantrum, but please, in the future, once we're at the family estate, I would ask you to stay within your own area of expertise."

My own area of expertise…

Would you like your eggs easy over or sunny-side up? And with a side order of opera or cabaret?

"Sure," Roxanna said, resisting the temptation to start mentally running through the list of antique rose varieties she'd been trying to memorize on the plane.

She noticed that Gino didn't specify who *we* was. Himself and Mrs. Gino Di Bartoli, she assumed. No prizes for guessing who the chief architect of the tantrum policy was, however. Hint—someone who didn't appear to understand bright, creative kids.

Someone who drove a Ferrari, she discovered a few minutes later.

A red Ferrari.

And who drove it fast.

Oh, it was wonderful! Rox didn't feel scared for a second. Gino drove to suit the conditions, and she'd seen the careful way he'd strapped his daughter into a child seat in the back before they started. On curvy or traffic-filled streets, he didn't attempt to weave between lanes or put his foot hard on the gas. Even the odd aggressive gesture or muttered curse were pretty restrained, compared to what Rox understood about Italian drivers.

When they hit the motorway heading to the north, however...

So cool.

She looked sideways at him, expecting to see a lazy grin of satisfaction, an enjoyment of the power and speed and sheer exhilaration, but no; his face still looked tight.

"Children grow out of tantrums," she blurted out, feeling stupidly responsible for the tight look and stupidly eager to make it go away.

Bleahh! Reason Number Eight. "You never think before you speak."

His mouth snapped open just far enough for speech. "They don't grow out of them if they've learned that tantrums are the secret to getting their own way."

"Does she ever get her own way?"

"No. As I said, we've been very strict about it. I should

say, Miss Cassidy has been very strict about it, since she is the one who has spent the most time with Pia."

Miss Cassidy.

Had to be the nanny.

Explained Pia's perfect English, with its occasional scary overtones of deceased British royalty.

Gino pronounced the nanny's name as Meess Cassi*di,* which was—so far—the only cute thing about him.

Once again failing to think before she spoke, Rox said, "I think sometimes a child needs to get her own way. She needs to know that people understand what's important to her. And she needs to learn…oh…how to tell the difference between the things she really wants and should have, and the things that are just a passing whim or in conflict with what others need. Isn't a blanket *no* just as bad as a blanket *yes?* Does anyone ever actually listen to her?"

Gino felt a steel band tighten around his head.

Had she made up her mind to sleep with Francesco? Did she think she was going to marry him? Was that why she'd suddenly shed her rabbity image and started offering opinions on issues that were none of her business? Did she think that they *were* her business now, because she was about to become a permanent part of the Di Bartoli family?

"I am not interested in discussing this with you any further, Dr. Madison."

Short silence.

"No. Of course. I'm sorry." She sounded more than sorry. She sounded chastened, as if she were really angry with herself. "I've been told before that I tend to do that."

"To interfere in things that aren't your business?"

"To speak first and think afterward. Foot-in-mouth disease."

"What? A disease!"

She was diseased? He was bringing her into his home with his precious daughter and she was—

"No, no. Oh, gosh! Language barrier. American slang. It's supposed to be funny. If you're tactless, if you say things you shouldn't have said, people say you've put your foot in your mouth. Foot-in-mouth disease. Get it?"

"Okay." He couldn't help grinning. Not so much at the allegedly humorous expression, but at her manic, anguished reaction to their misunderstanding.

"I'm so sorry if I gave you a heart attack there!" She was wincing and flapping her hands, clasping them together, begging him to understand, acting sincerely distressed. "I do that. I say things. And—oh my gosh! My blouse isn't even done up right. You're never going to beli—" She stopped, then fastened the slipped-through button that had caught his attention when she'd first come up to him in the terminal.

"Never going to what?" he asked.

He was curious.

And he'd started to have a theoretical inkling about what Francesco might have seen in her.

There was a beat of silence.

"Never going to forgive me," she said.

"Don't be ridiculous. It was a small misunderstanding."

"No, um, I meant for my comments about the t-a-n-t-r-u-m thing." She spelled out the critical word.

"I will forgive you if it's not mentioned again."

"Right. Okay. It won't be." She stopped flapping and clasping her hands, settled a little deeper into her seat and turned to look out of the window.

Glancing in the rearview mirror, Gino saw that Pia

had fallen asleep. It was three-thirty in the afternoon. They'd be home in an hour and a half. If she slept until then, she'd be difficult to settle tonight, and he was essentially on his own. Miss Cassidy was taking a four-week paid break in England, at his request. It was the right thing, he was sure of it, yet he felt daunted.

Even utterly capable, immaculate, Paris-born Angele had been daunted by taking care of Pia. Gino and Angele had separated when Pia was just six months old, and of course she had gone with her mother—and with Miss Cassidy, whom they'd hired before their baby was even born. Miss Cassidy had been part of the divorce settlement, if you wanted to look at it that way, a live-in fixture at the spacious apartment Angele had rented in Rome.

During Angele's illness two years ago…such an aggressive form of cancer… Gino hated to think about it…he'd moved Pia and Miss Cassidy back into his own apartment, but he hadn't changed anything about their routine. He hadn't felt it was his place. He had consulted with Angele's older sister Lisette, also married to an Italian and based in Rome, and she had agreed.

"Of course, you must think of what my sister would have done and what she would have wanted!"

"I need you to help me with all of that, Lisette."

"I'm here, Gino. You know I am."

Pia had lost her mother. Miss Cassidy gave her continuity of care and affection. Gino himself had been very tied up with the acquisition of a rival company that year and with his complicated feelings about his ex-wife's death. He worked long hours, and he traveled frequently.

"I'm not sure how much Francesco has told you

about my situation," he suddenly said, dragging Roxanna Madison's rapt attention from the unfolding views of Tuscany in early spring.

As a horticultural expert, it made sense that she was enthralled. He should probably have left her in peace. But with Pia safely asleep and with the prospect of the three of them living under the same roof for several weeks, he wanted to make sure everything was clear. And he wanted it to come from him, not from Francesco over the phone, or from the staff employed at the Di Bartoli *palazzo* and surrounding tract of land.

"Um, not much," she answered.

So he told her about Angele, Miss Cassidy, the apartment in Rome and his own growing belief, over the past few months, that he needed to get more involved with Pia, get more of an idea about the reason behind the tantrums. Was it because of her mother's death? Was there some area in which her needs were not being met? He was her father. It was his duty to understand his little girl.

"Thank you for sharing that with me," Roxanna said when he'd finished speaking, and he realized he'd gotten more personal and detailed than he'd intended and that he'd shown more vulnerability also.

It didn't make sense. On top of the two narrow misses on major tantrums, those few moments of fearing that he'd lost Pia at the airport must have unsettled him more than he'd thought.

Still thinking about his daughter, he made the final turn into the graveled avenue that led to the estate, and the *palazzo* came into view, its terra-cotta-tiled roof softly washed by the thin late-afternoon March sunshine, and the first hints of spring green dusting the landscape all around.

"Ohhh, it's beautiful!" Dr. Madison said beside him. "I mean, today. It looks particularly beautiful today. Compared to when I was last here, last week, when it was, when it was—"

"Probably raining," he finished for her, not really thinking about it.

Pia was still asleep, and he wondered how disastrous the consequences would be later on tonight if he left her that way, parked safely in front of the *palazzo* with the car windows open. Or should he wake her up at once? He knew from recent experience that this would definitely make her cry.

Chapter Two

In her room at midnight that night, Rox very much wanted to call Rowie and Mom to report, like a covert operative, that she'd achieved successful and undetected insertion into the target zone. She'd managed to greet Maria, the housekeeper, as if the two of them had met before. She'd correctly matched the three gardeners' names with the descriptions of them that Row had given her. She'd used the sketchy map of the *palazzo*'s interior to navigate her way to her bedroom, and had only gotten lost once.

But Rowie and Mom were on the plane to Florida, so she couldn't.

At least, she really hoped they were on the plane to Florida. What if Row couldn't bring herself to leave the hotel, even when she had Mom with her every step of the way?

How much of the difference in their personalities

came down to the fact that Rox had been born first and heaviest and healthiest and easiest? It had always seemed to her like such a random quirk of fate. She'd held the winning ticket in that particular lottery, and she wasn't going to let her sister suffer for it.

Since she couldn't call Mom and Rowie, she called Dad instead. "You haven't heard from them?"

"No, which means they must be safely on the plane." He sounded relieved about it, also.

"That's great! Tell Rowie as soon as you see her that everything is going fine here, no problems, and she's not to worry about a thing. She's to focus on herself, on getting the right therapist and the right treatment, and getting better."

"Will do, honey."

"Talk to you soon."

"Thanks for doing this for your sister."

"Oh, it's a walk in the park, it's a breeze," Rox lied. "It's going to be fun. Make sure she really knows she doesn't have to worry about me."

Roxanna didn't feel sleepy, since her body was still set on New Jersey time. When Gino had taken his still-wide-awake and protesting daughter up to bed an hour ago, Rox had almost blurted out something about jet lag and understanding how Pia felt. She'd shut her treacherous mouth just in time.

You weren't supposed to get jet lag going from London to Italy, since their time zones were only an hour apart, so she'd put on a fake yawn, said good-night, and hidden her raring-to-go energy levels in this gorgeous, high-ceilinged, powder-blue-painted room, with adjoining bathroom, that Francesco had assigned to her sister.

It was no coincidence, Roxanna knew, that the room was situated just along the corridor from where Francesco had slept. She wondered whether Rowie might have been able to hold herself together here in Italy, enough to complete the garden project, if she hadn't faced Francesco's constant and seductive attempts to sleep with her.

Water under the bridge now.

Rox had other, more urgent things to think about.

She would have to study Rowena's plant lists, work schedules, delivery dates and garden bed layouts for a few hours until she really got sleepy. And there was no alarm clock in the room, so she'd have to leave the painted wooden shutters open and trust to the morning light to wake her at an hour that wasn't suspiciously late.

Considering that she didn't feel tired, Rox found it hard to concentrate on the pages of notes Rowena had given her in London, or on the bundle of stuff she'd sneaked up to her room from the sunny and spacious office Rowena had been given downstairs. She loved flowers and shrubs and gardens, sure, but not the way Rowie did, not on the same level of detail. She loved beautiful vistas, dramatic groupings of color, and sweet, heady scents...

But did she really need to know exactly what quantity of *Souvenir de la Malmaison, Belle de Crecy, Eglantine, Celsiana* and a dozen other varieties of rose Row had ordered for the Pink Walk? Did she need to know that crested moss was also known as *Chapeau de Napoleon?*

Cram, cram, cram.

Exam tomorrow.

Concentrate, Rox!

Instead, her mind kept straying to Gino and his daughter. They made such a gorgeous pair, with their dark coloring, their lashes as thick as sable paintbrushes, their satin-smooth olive skin, their impeccable bone structure.

You could have photographed them at a pavement café or in a cobbled town square for one of those evocative postcards of Italian street life that looked like a black-and-white movie still from the era of the young Sophia Loren…if you could have gotten arrogant, supersuccessful Gino to stop frowning at Pia and looking so totally at sea about his daughter.

The little girl had been difficult tonight, Rox had to admit. Pia wouldn't sit properly at the big dining room table to eat—Roxanna had thought the food was fabulous—but had just wanted to run around and play. Afterward, she seemed bored with her fancy, pristine dolls. She darted into some vast, echoing formal sitting room—the *salone,* they seemed to call it—lifted the lid on the grand piano and started to tinkle the keys. When she got into trouble for it, instead of stopping she pounded them harder and harder.

Had a great sense of rhythm, actually.

She had been physically removed from the instrument and then from the room, and she had started to kick and scream. Gino had looked embarrassed, upset and at the end of his rope. His vulnerability called forth an odd connection to him that Roxanna didn't think she could have felt with a man like that in any other situation. She didn't like the commanding type, and she ought to know, since she'd been married to one for six years.

As the tantrum had unravelled, Maria the housekeeper clearly hadn't known whether to step in or say nothing. Rox had felt seriously out of place. She had mumbled something about going for a walk, even though it was dark outside by that time.

Back and forth along a terrace she had gone, then round and round a beautiful old fountain that hadn't yet been restored. The place was fabulous with its air of age-tarnished grandeur and luxury. Inside, she had still been able to hear Pia letting loose. When silence finally had descended and she had ventured back indoors, she had found the little girl up at the polished rosewood table where she should have been an hour earlier, face sticky with ice cream, screaming forgotten, mood utterly content.

Oh, so we never give in to Pia's tantrums, do we?

Not very fair of her to gloat over it like that, when Gino looked as if he'd aged ten years in the process.

She didn't usually gloat.

Harlan hadn't even mentioned it on his list.

And now, here in her big, silent bedroom, she couldn't stop thinking about Gino, wondering how he'd dug himself into such a hole, wishing too strongly that she could help, knowing that she never could. A man like that wouldn't let her.

She didn't get to sleep until after four.

Was Dr. Madison ever going to wake up?

Gino had passed a sleepless night himself, but he'd risen at eight. Now it was ten and there was still no sign of her. He'd scheduled a part of the morning for touring the garden together, with her plans in hand, but if she didn't appear soon, the morning would be gone. He didn't feel comfortable about rapping on her door to waken her since they hadn't agreed on a starting time, but he was getting annoyed.

Meanwhile, he tried to get some work done, but that wasn't much of a success.

He'd naively imagined that he could put on a DVD for Pia, which she would watch quietly in the background while he made business calls, sent e-mails and worked on his laptop. But Pia had seen the DVD movie before.

"Sixteen times!" she said.

And she certainly seemed to know the songs in it by heart.

He tried to settle her with a book instead, but she wanted him to read it with her. "Because I can't read."

"Can't you look at the pictures?"

"I want to read the words. With you."

He read the words with her.

Actually, she almost could read on her own. She knew all of her letters, and when there was an easy word like *boo* or *cat*—it was a book in English—she could sound it out with his help. He felt a stirring of pride, found an Italian book and tried that with her, and she did just as well. He must ask Miss Cassidy how much time she'd spent on this sort of thing with Pia.

All the same, both books together only occupied twenty minutes, and when they were finished, she was bored again. He began to follow her from room to room, hoping she'd settle on something and racking his brain about a new strategy.

Should he hire a temporary nanny? He could easily go through an agency and have someone in place by the beginning of next week. But wouldn't that defeat his whole purpose of getting to understand Pia better? He'd been frustrated in recent months by Miss Cassidy's staged, formal and prearranged sessions of father-daughter time, with Pia always freshly bathed and fed, and outfitted like the window display at a Parisian fashion boutique.

Anyhow, here was Dr. Madison at last, dressed in her garden clothes—khaki stretch pants and a fleecy zippered top in a slightly lighter shade. The zipper was only pulled halfway up, showing a white T-shirt that looked a little too tight—the kind of tight that no man would ever complain about. Beneath it, her very nice breasts bounced as she hurried down the stairs.

"Good morning, uh, Rowena," he said. He'd asked her weeks ago to call him Gino, and she did, but for some reason he found it hard to reciprocate with her first name today, and kept thinking of her by her formal title of Dr. Madison, instead.

"Good morning… Oh, but I am so sorry!" she gasped, radiating remorse like electrical energy. "I don't know what can have made me sleep in like that! If it's possible for me to have an alarm clock in the room, I would appreciate it, because I really do not want this to happen again!"

Her cheeks were flushed. Her hair was damp at the ends. If she'd brushed it just now, she hadn't done a very good job, because it was all over the place, like the hair of a woman caught in bed with her lover.

"That's fine," Gino answered. "I've been reading with Pia. The alarm clock is a good idea, however."

He couldn't find the right tone. He was annoyed, yes, but at the same time he had an image of those rounded, bouncing breasts in his mind, wondering if they were a big part of the attraction for Francesco.

He'd begun to understand that Dr. Madison did have some good…uh…features, surprisingly.

He also wanted to grin in sheer appreciation of the energy she gave off. He hadn't noticed that, the other times they'd met. She'd been so focused on her scrupulously researched lists of rose varieties and their history. She'd seemed to direct too much of her energy inward and had been a little colorless to his eye.

"Would you like some breakfast before we start?" he offered.

"Um, if it's not too much trouble."

It was.

Far too much trouble.

Another delay in his already shattered morning.

But he couldn't ask her to tramp around the gardens with him on an empty stomach, so…

"I'll call Maria, and you can tell her what you would like. There may still be coffee on the sideboard in the dining room. Will you excuse me while I make some phone calls? Come along, Pia."

"If they're business calls, why don't I keep Pia with me?" Dr. Madison suggested quickly. "Pia, you can pour my juice and tell me what breakfast foods are called in Italian. You can be my teacher. Would that be nice?"

Gino held his breath, waiting for *No, I wanna go with Papa,* and wondering whether his saying *Okay, come with me, then* would count as immediate capitulation to a tantrum that hadn't quite happened yet but surely would if he insisted she was to go with Dr. Madison.

"Yes! It would be delightful!" Pia said and reeled off several breakfast words in Italian.

"You might have to go a little slower than that, Your

Majesty, and you might have to get quite strict with me when I make silly mistakes. I think I'm going to be a very bad student!"

Pia laughed. She was already halfway to the dining room, her hand stretched out to take Dr. Madison's, which was reaching back to her, open and inviting. The horticultural expert looked across at Gino, raised her eyebrows and grinned at him as if to say, "Didn't I handle that well!"

He grinned back, too surprised not to, even though the grin felt…rusty.

Yes, I have to admit, you handled it well.

Then he let the grin drop and went to get some work done.

It was well after eleven when he surfaced from negotiating an unexpected problem in the Paris office and realized that even if Dr. Madison had ordered a full American breakfast, she must have finished eating it by now and must have learned by heart every Italian breakfast word Pia could think of to teach her. He went in search of them, clued in to their whereabouts by the sound of the piano that Pia had gotten into so much trouble over last night.

Dr. Madison had taught Pia to play "Chopsticks."

As a duet.

With the doctor herself improvising some impressive, wild-fingered variations in the bass.

"Now we're going to do it sad, Pia," Gino heard her say. He paused in the doorway. "Listen, stop for a minute, can you hear me slowing down? Can you hear me changing the notes?" She went into a minor key. "Does it sound sadder to you now? Can you play it sad with me? Oh, boohoo, our chopsticks are bro-o-o-ken. Oh, it's tragic, it's terrible, we're so, so sad, our notes are going so slowly, our fingers are so heavy on the keys, boohoo."

He came farther into the room and she caught sight of him, nodded to show that she understood he was ready for their tour.

"Pia, someone's fixed our chopsticks!" she said. "We're happy again. We can get fast. Our fingers are moving so fast we can't see them. I'm chasing you. Can you play as fast as me? I'm catching up, go faster, Pia. Faster, faster!"

Pia's playing collapsed into laughter and fractured rhythm and thumping keys, and Dr. Madison sank sideways against her little shoulder in an exaggerated parody of breathlessness and exhaustion after a race.

"There! Whew! Fabulous! Thank you! It's not nearly as much fun playing 'Chopsticks' on my own. Do you remember what this note is called, Pia?" She touched a key, and the sound of a single note vibrated from the instrument.

"Middle C," Pia said.

"That's right. Now if I shut the piano lid and open it again, can you still find Middle C?" She did as she'd described, and Pia's finger went straight to the right note. "Very good!" She stood up, closed the lid once more, and turned to Gino. "We're ready. I'm sorry, I felt I should—"

"No, that's fine. You're right. You needed to finish properly. Pia, Dr. Madison is going to show us her plans for the garden, now."

Crunch time, Roxanna thought.

She'd decided to wing it without Rowena's written and sketched-out plans, because she knew that her sister would have had the whole thing locked down in her memory the way Rox had locked down the lyrics and music to all her favorite songs. Without those comforting scrolls of paper clutched in her hands, however, she felt like an actress caught without a vital prop.

Gino was dressed down today, in a white Polo shirt that showed off the natural tan on his arms and on that very nicely shaped column of neck appearing from inside the Polo collar. He wore his hair short at the back, but not too short; just the right length for a woman's fingers to run through—not too prickly, not too soft.

Rox happened to be an authority on exactly what this length was, because she'd never convinced Harlan to let his hair grow to it. He'd always kept it as short as cornfield stubble.

After she'd retrieved some of Rowie's notes from the office, Gino led the way outside, and asked her about what she'd been doing with Pia. "Was it a lesson, or just fun?"

And that was a much safer subject than either garden restoration or the best length for a man's hair, so she snatched it up.

With too much enthusiasm, as usual.

"Lessons and fun should be the same thing for a four-year-old, I think, especially with something like music, if you don't want to put them off for life. So it was both, really. And she was very responsive. She was great!"

"Really?" He sounded skeptical, as if he didn't dare to hope for too much where his daughter was concerned. And that was just ridiculous!

"Gino, she's a very bright, creative little girl, hungry

to learn. She latched on to what we were doing incredibly fast, and she loved it. I think you should consider music lessons for her."

He thought about it for a minute, then shook his head. "When she's older."

Oh, okay, right.

Older.

You mean, when she's snowed under with schoolwork. When that great big spark of joy and curiosity has been completely snuffed out by gray dresses and repressive tantrum control. When you can hit her with endless scales and finger exercises, and toss poor old Beethoven's trampled-on "Fur Elise" at her like tossing a bone.

Makes total sense.

But, as we discussed yesterday, it's none of my business, so I'll keep my trap shut.

"You're very talented at music, by the way," he added, distracting her.

"Oh…not half as talented as I'd like to be. I love it, but, no, I'm coming to realize—"

That Harlan is probably right about my voice.

Oops, and that Harlan has nothing to do with any of this, because I'm pretending to be my twin sister.

"Gardens are my real love, of course," she quickly added.

"Talk me through the whole plan," he invited her.

Examination time.

Half an hour later, she was pretty confident she'd earned a passing grade. When you had to do all your exam preparation the night before, jet lag did have its advantages. Walking around the extensive and beautiful but dilapidated and overgrown old gardens, only part of which had yet been cleared under Rowena's supervision, they managed the odd snatch of polite but slightly more personal conversation, also, which made Rox relax more than she'd expected to.

She asked Gino whether he had any kind of a garden in Rome, and he told her, "Only the one in the oil painting on my wall. It's from the French Impressionist school. Not by a world-famous artist, but pretty." He asked her why she'd chosen to go into a field like this. The combination of dry historical research and outdoor work was unusual, wasn't it?

And since Roxanna knew her twin sister so well, she could find an answer that was true for Row and true for herself, as well. Something about how you can appreciate and enjoy something more when there's more than one layer to it. A seven-foot-high *Harrison's Yellow* rosebush in full bloom is beautiful all on its own when you're standing in front of it on a gorgeous day, but when you also know that pioneers on the Oregon Trail packed the same rose in their wagons to plant out west…Well, that adds something, doesn't it?

She didn't express it very well. Rambled on a sentence or two too long, no doubt. Reasons Number One and Two, by the way: "You're always so (expletive deleted) enthusiastic," and "You never know when to stop talking."

But this morning she was supposed to talk, so she did, and Gino listened, while Pia played in sunshine that definitely felt as if it were part of spring today.

"Impressive," Gino said, when Rox had finished.

Was that an A grade?

Sounded like an A.

She relaxed a little too much, and that mouth of hers opened right up and she said, "Of course, if it were me, I'd do it the other way around."

Gino looked at her blankly. "But it is you."

"I mean, if it were my garden, if I weren't working for you, the client. Fulfilling your—"

Help, help, help!

Why did I say it?

"Tell me what you're talking about." He frowned, sounded impatient. "The other way around?"

They stood at the end of a long, south-facing wall that marched along the side of the formal part of the garden, edged by a gravel track and overlooking a sloping field of vines that were just showing the first hints of green growth. Pia was throwing bits of gravel toward the vines. It was a very pretty spot, but since they were on the far side of the wall, it wasn't visible from the main garden, the terrace or the house.

Rox had just finished dutifully describing to Gino how she—i.e. Rowena, as per Rowena's plans—envisaged a single line of roses growing all along the wall, chosen not for their heritage value, like those in the main garden, but for other features, such as color and scent. And now, instead of leaving it at that, Rox had gone and blurted out her own opinion.

Harlan's Reason Number Three: "You have an opinion about everything."

"Well…" she said cautiously. Was there a way she could get out of this? Backtrack? Fob Gino off? No. She'd already put one foot in it. She had no choice now but to jump in with both. "I just mean that, even though, historically, the antique roses would obviously have been a part of the main garden, I think it could work better to have them along this wall instead."

"Yes?" Gino said, indicating that she should please continue to insert her feet even deeper.

"Um, you see, initially, conforming to…uh…what I thought the family wanted, I attempted to combine the…uh…botanical-historical dimension of the main garden with the…uh…aesthetic dimension, but in some ways this may well mean that neither goal is effectively fulfilled. Whereas—"

She took a breath.

A very large, shuddery and somewhat desperate breath.

"—if we were to treat this wall as a kind of time line, we could create quite a fascinating walking history lesson on the development of rose species, dating from sixteenth-century varieties such as *Eglantine* and *Austrian Copper* and—and—" Yikes! "—*Maiden's Blush…*" Whew! "…through to the hybrid teas cultivated since, um, 1867—" Was that date right? "—going from one end of the wall to the other. And that would mean we could leave the main garden as an exercise in pure drama." She stopped channeling Rowie for a minute and dropped right into Rox. "And I love drama in a garden, don't you?"

Harlan's Reason Number Four: "You always think other people will agree with you."

"Color and scent and big, showy effects," she went on, knowing it was too late to stop now, so she might as well sell the idea as best she could. "A garden you can really breathe and see and feel and be passionate about."

Gino looked blank again.

He was good at that.

Blank, arrogant shock at the fact that other people were so much slower to grasp things than he was. "Then why didn't you plan it that way in the first place?" he said.

Rox's turn at doing the blank look. "You mean you like the idea?"

"Yes. Very much. You're right. We should keep the history and the drama separate. Why haven't you suggested this before?"

"I—I thought—at the meeting—you wanted—"

"I don't remember saying so."

"Well, Francesco…"

"Hmm, possibly Francesco might have, but I doubt he gave it much thought. Look, is it too late to do it this new way? The other way around, as you put it? Would it drastically change which roses you've ordered, and how many, and your timetable for planting?"

Yikes, again.

How should I know?

"I—I'd have to check my notes."

And call Row.

Even if it is, what, around six in the morning in Florida.

"Do that, then, and get back to me with your answer as soon as possible. I like the new idea better."

He was already moving toward the house, calling Pia's name over his shoulder as he went. Pia didn't come. She was still throwing bits of gravel. "Pia, it's time to come in now," he said more sternly. "And I will not have any nonsense about it!"

The pale gravel looked like fallen blossom on the brown earth beside the vines. Pia picked up another piece, scowling just like her daddy.

"Go in," Gino told Rox. His mouth had gone tight. "I'll handle this."

Back at the *palazzo,* from which Pia's frustrated screams could barely be heard, the housekeeper told Roxanna that there was a phone message waiting for her.

Whew! In Florida, Rowie was up early. Rox could call her right back and learn just how deep a hole she'd dug herself into.

"From Francesco," Maria said.

"I'll, uh, phone him from my room."

Once I've thumbed frantically through Rowena's notes to find his number in Rome. I know she wrote it down for me somewhere...

"Hi-i-i, Francesco!"

"You're back? It's so good to hear your voice." His breath swept heavily into her ear through the earpiece of the phone. "I left you alone while you were in London, I knew you needed time. But I've missed you, the way a thirsty flower misses rain. Have you missed me, sweetheart?"

"I've been thinking about you..." True, but not the way he thought.

"And have you made a decision?"

"About..." Rox let the word hang, hoping he'd fill in the blank for her, even though she was pretty sure what decision he was talking about.

And it didn't involve roses.

Instead, he took her hesitation as an answer he didn't want. "Haven't I given you long enough? More than long enough? Let me tell you, my darling little American, there comes a point where a woman's holding back stops increasing a man's interest and becomes only annoying."

Annoying?

Annoying?

Roxanna thought about the long, tearful session she'd had with Rowie in London, when they should have been talking detail on the Di Bartoli garden. She thought about all of Row's doubt, her anguished questions about what she really felt and what Francesco really wanted. She unfortunately didn't think about whether opening her mouth and speaking her mind might endanger the very contract she'd come here to protect.

Francesco had a fiancée, dang him. He'd said all these fervent, romantic, irresistible European-type things to Rowena, but did he love her? Really? Would he put his money where his mouth was and break it off with Marcellina? Did Rowena want him to?

"I just can't, Rox," Rowie had said in London. "I can't give him what he wants. I—I don't think he means any of it. N-not really. I'm so confused. I want him to mean it, but in my heart…"

And Francesco had no clue about the anxiety disorder, no clue about Row's strong principles, her sweet, naive belief in a perfect happy-ever-after, her pretzel-like attempts to please everyone she cared about and her determination not to hurt his fiancée, a woman she hadn't even met, and dismissed all of this as merely *annoying?*

"You want an answer right now?" Rox asked him.

"I am hungry for it! I am hungry for you. Marcellina means nothing to me. I will marry her, yes, of course, because, you understand, it is what I owe my family, but you will always be—"

"Okay, here's my answer. Go take a flying leap! Is that enough of a decision for you?"

"Rowena…?"

"Go take a flying flip at the moon, Francesco Di Bartoli. Clear now?"

With a tingling, light-headed sense of satisfaction, Roxanna slammed down the phone.

Chapter Three

"So…I, um, said no to Francesco for you, Rowie."

They'd already discussed the major change to the design concept of the garden. At just after six on a Thursday morning in Florida, Rowena had been a little taken aback, but then she'd quickly seized on the idea and gotten inspired.

She hadn't thought to go so far beyond the original design, but she loved the idea of a historical time line, and yes, it should only make a small difference to which roses she'd ordered. She could tell Roxanna exactly what changes would be required, and she'd only need to make one follow-up call to each of the two specialist rose nurseries.

Meanwhile, she could work on creating bilingual plaques in Italian and English describing the history of each antique variety. The information could be tied in to historical developments in cosmetics and medicine, making that part of the garden a showpiece for visiting business associates of the Di Bartoli Corporation. *Rosa gallica officinalis,* for example, was used for medicinal purposes for centuries, as well as for perfume-making.

If Rowena did some more research on the subject…

After just a few minutes, she had sounded so much more energetic and confident than she'd been in London, only two days ago. She really loved her work, loved those dusty libraries and archives, those steamy greenhouses and rows of young plants. If she could find a good therapist who could help her get the rest of her life under control, she'd soon find a man who deserved her way more than Francesco Di Bartoli did.

Rox held her breath, waiting for her sister's reaction to what she'd said about her own recent phone conversation with the man.

"Oh, you did? An absolute, one hundred percent no?" Rowie said.

"Um, yes. Pretty much one hundred percent, I'd say."

Okay, she really had to breathe now. Before this next bit. The bit that might have Francesco arguing to his older brother that the American garden expert should be sacked on the spot and replaced with someone who had a more appropriate idea of her humble place in the Di Bartoli universe.

"The phone slam kind of emphasized my point," she finished.

"You slammed down the phone?"

"Uh, yeah."

Don't yell at me about it, Rowie…

Rowie would never yell. "Oh, thank you!" she said.

"It's…it's for the best. I could never really have given him what he wanted."

Rowena hadn't yet thought about the professional implications. Rox decided not to scare her now, when there was still a chance that Francesco might let the phone slam go.

"No, Row!" she said instead. "He could never have given *you* what *you* wanted! Or what you deserved!" She sketched out her phone conversation with Gino's younger brother in more detail, including his convenient little plan for marrying wealthy and well-connected Marcellina but keeping Rowena for some fun on the side. "I told him to take a flying leap! Just before the phone slam part."

Rowie laughed. "Wow! Let me picture that moment in my head." She laughed again. Then she sighed. "Oh well, it was flattering while it lasted."

"Flattering? But not shattering?"

"Yeah, shattering, too. He said so many wonderful things to me. I—I thought…I—I wanted… Even though I only believed half of them, half was enough. It's good to be with Mom and Dad. I have a journey I need to make now. I can see that. I'm going to start looking for the right therapist on Monday."

"Love you, Rowie."

"Love you, too, Rox."

Gino carried Pia in through the front door. She was still screaming. Echoing against the high ceilings and stone floor of the *palazzo,* the sound seemed even louder than it had outside next to the vines. He had bruised shins from Pia's flailing legs and a battered heart because of his own sense of failure.

How could a grown man be reduced to such a raw-nerved mass of self-doubt by one little girl?

Maria approached cautiously. "You want me to take her, Signor Di Bartoli?" She'd had seven children of her own, and now she was a grandmother twelve times over and counting. She knew just a little bit about kids.

But pride wouldn't let Gino take the easy way out today, the way he had done last night when Maria had suggested ice cream.

"I'll handle it," he said. Or shouted, rather. So he could be heard above the screams. "We're going up to her room."

"Francesco phoned."

"I'll call him back."

"For Dr. Madison."

"Ah."

There was no point in trying for a more detailed conversation with this level of noise. He got Pia to her room and grimly held on to her, his arms tight enough to stop her from hurting herself but not so tight that he could possibly hurt her. It took an hour for her to exhaust herself into silence and then sleep. Gino tucked her into bed, under a crisp white sheet and a light cotton blanket, then watched her peaceful, angelic little face.

"This is not going to happen again," he muttered. "I am not going to handle it this way. It can't be right. Can it, little girl?"

He bent and kissed her, then tiptoed out of the room. He had no alternative strategy in place, but at least he'd thrown out the one that clearly wasn't working.

Downstairs, he found a late lunch waiting, and Dr. Madison seated at the dining table, just about to eat it. He sat down opposite, meters from her across the expanse of polished rosewood, hoping his appetite would revive at the first tastes of green salad, fresh bread and Maria's bean and pasta soup.

"I've looked at my notes, and we can make the changes without anything more than a few small revisions to what I've ordered," the American woman told him.

"That's great." He knew he hadn't managed a shred of enthusiasm, and that he must look exhausted.

Dr. Madison, in contrast, looked to be actually sizzling with energy. It glowed from within, lighting up the rich blue of her eyes and painting a color on her cheeks that could have matched one of her beloved roses.

That's right, Gino remembered. She had talked to Francesco just now. What had he said? *Something to flatter and excite her, I can see that.*

"Is Pia all right?" she asked, as if Francesco weren't on her mind.

"She's asleep."

"Well, we'd all be, after a performance like that, poor little sweetheart!"

"So you think she should be pitied, not punished?"

"You're not interested in my opinion, are you?"

"Why would I ask for it if I wasn't interested in it?"

"Because yesterday you told me it was none of my business. You must be more desperate today." She raised her eyebrows at him, as if daring him to challenge her outrageous cheekiness.

"You're very happy to speak your mind, aren't you?"

In fact, how long had it been since *anyone* had dared or wanted to act cheeky with him? Cheeky just hadn't been in Angele's repertoire at all. She'd been as cool and smooth as thick cream, her behavior poised, sophisticated and perfect on every occasion.

"So I've been told," Rowena Madison said.

"By many people, I expect."

"By my ex-husband, mainly."

Oh, so she had one of those, too. Did Francesco know? He usually preferred a woman not to have complications of that kind.

"And you think your ex-husband was wrong?" Gino didn't really know why he was pushing this conversation topic.

For Francesco's benefit?

"No, I'm sure he was right. He was right in most of the things he said about me. He was…you know…one of those people who are a bit too perfect themselves."

"How boring!" Gino said, without thinking too much about his response. He didn't have time. Dr. Madison was speaking again already.

"No! Not boring at all! Like walking on a knife edge. You can't describe that as boring. Far too nerve-racking, always waiting, holding my breath, until I made the next mistake."

"And so you left."

"He left," Rox corrected. "When I made what he decided was one mistake too many."

Reason Number Twenty-one. Like all the others, she knew it by heart. "You forgot to pick up my six-hundred-dollar ski jacket from the cleaner six months ago, and now they've gone out of business and their unclaimed stock has been sold off to pay creditors and that, Rox, is the (expletive deleted) end, as far as I'm concerned. It's over."

Naively, Rox hadn't realized that there was also another woman in the picture until Harlan had already moved in with her.

"I left Angele," Gino said. Then one of those hell-did-I-really-say-that-out-loud-what's-wrong-with-me looks appeared on his face.

"Because she made too many mistakes?"

Had to be a reason like that, Rox decided before Gino answered. Not that he reminded her of Harlan in any way, but he was definitely the born-to-command type. He would surround himself with ultracompetency, even in a wife. He wouldn't want slapdash, inconsistent, emotional, forgetful, any of that.

"No, because I was…we were both…bored."

"You should have taken up a hobby together. Pottery." He wasn't impressed. "Parachuting?" Glimmer of a reaction. "Illicit dealing in nuclear arms!"

He laughed. *Gotcha!*

Rox liked it when she could make a man laugh.

Especially when he had a gorgeous smile, which, by pure coincidence, Gino did. It crinkled up his eyes, spread all over his face and showed off his even white teeth. "I hadn't thought of a shared hobby," he murmured. Then he frowned and suddenly looked older, and Rox remembered that it was too late for hobbies as a marriage-fixing strategy now.

Pia's mother had died.

"It must have been very difficult," she said. "I can understand how hard it must be for all of you to find the right approach with your daughter. And I know this is none of my business, but—"

"So far that hasn't stopped you," he pointed out.

"Uh, exactly."

"You're honest!"

"So I might as well come right out and say it. You have a lot going for you...some women would think." Sounded like an insult. "Many women," she revised. "If remarriage was anywhere on your horizon, that might make things easier with Pia. A woman's touch. And, man or woman, it's difficult for anyone raising a child on their own."

"No," Gino answered, sounding very decisive. "There's no possibility of my marrying again. I couldn't make it work the first time, even with someone as incredible as Angele. I'm not taking the risk a second time."

And that's one of the four trillion ways in which we're completely different, Rox thought. *Because I'd get married again in a heartbeat, if I could find the right man and if I believed that he wanted me for the right reasons.*

There was a little silence, then Gino said, "How about you?" Roxanna was taken by surprise a bit, because she was the busybody around this place, not him.

"You mean, would I ever get married again?"

"Yes."

"It would take a very special kind of man," she said, adding inwardly, *the kind who's not that fussy.* "But, yes, if I could find him, if I loved him, if he loved me, if he...oh...knew who I really was, I'd marry him."

"That's good. I admire your faith."

"Thank you. I think."

Silence.

Chinking of antique silver spoons in wide antique Italian ceramic soup bowls.

Deep unspoken mutual regret about extent of personal revelations.

Definite change in emotional atmosphere—temperature drop of at least ten degrees.

Gino looked up from his empty soup bowl after several minutes to see that the garden expert had finished eating, too. He wondered what had possessed him, just now, to seek Rowena Madison's opinion, to give away so much and to ask her all those questions about her own life, her attitudes and her past.

There were only two possible reasons that made sense.

Because he'd lost all judgment and control, thanks to his battles with Pia, or because he wanted to work out what was really going on between this woman and his brother. Who was manipulating the situation to their own advantage? Who was using whom?

"Did you have a good talk with Francesco?" he asked deliberately. "Maria told me he'd called."

"A very good talk, thanks." A smile slipped onto her face—secretive, satisfied.

Something kicked inside him, an emotional jolt that he didn't understand. He felt angry, suddenly. What had she gotten Francesco to agree to? An expensive gift? An illicit vacation? Worst of all, an end to his engagement?

It would be a disaster if Francesco married this American instead of Marcellina!

Marcellina understood her fiancé, knew his weaknesses and managed them well. They had the prospect of a successful thirty- or forty-year marriage, with an appropriate number of children, in which Marcellina would turn a blind eye to some of Francesco's faults and come down on others like an elephant on an ant.

With Marcellina at his side, Francesco could safely be given a key executive role in the family corporation. Without her, he would mess up in so many areas, Gino didn't even want to think about it.

Rowena Madison couldn't possibly succeed in marriage with a man like Francesco. She had more spirit than Gino had given her credit for at their previous meetings, yet in some ways she was naive. Too open. Too extravagant in what she felt. She needed someone who took responsibility for his own actions, who was looking for light and life and energy, not for the business partnership style of marriage that Francesco needed.

But a smile still softened her full lips and it definitely belonged to a woman who was happy with the state of things between herself and her lover. The smile wasn't accompanied by dewy eyes, either. It didn't look like that of a woman who was genuinely smitten—far too cool for that.

She thinks she's in control, Gino thought. *She thinks she has Francesco just where she wants him. And she's definitely not in love.*

He felt quite sure about all of this, but he was never satisfied by conclusions based on instinct alone. He liked to check his facts and test his theories. How could he test this one? How could he get rid of a nagging sense that something didn't fit?

Maria brought the espresso pot to the table and he poured himself a tiny cup of coffee so dark and strong it could almost lift the spoon. Across the table, Rowena

Madison shook her head, and he told her, "Don't wait, then. I know you have work to do."

He sat over his coffee for longer than usual after she'd gone.

Roxanna didn't see Gino all afternoon. She knew he must be working, too, because he had an office with shuttered doors that opened onto the terrace and the day was warm enough that he'd opened the window. Walking past a couple of times, she heard his voice speaking into the phone and the hum of a printer. She also knew that Maria was entertaining Pia in the kitchen, making sweet treats as well as the evening meal.

Rox had gotten instructions from Rowena over the phone about what to tell the team of three gardeners who were working under her supervision, and Row had also advised, "Get your own hands dirty, because I always do!" She came in at five, as the shadows were lengthening across the vineyards, feeling tired and cold and filthy. Nice kind of filthy. As Row always said, "It's just good, clean dirt."

The shower felt wonderful. It cleaned out every pore and relaxed every muscle. Afterward, however, standing in front of the large, old-fashioned closet with a towel wrapped around her, Roxanna didn't know what to wear. Rowie's clothes never felt quite right, and it wasn't just because of their slightly tighter fit on her slightly fuller frame.

She knew she was supposed to team either the matching pink-beige skirt and jacket with the cream silk shell blouse, or the black trousers with the blue cotton sweater, but one outfit seemed too formal and the other too plain. A couple of other possibilities languished in the laundry hamper in her private bathroom. She ended up choosing the trousers and wearing the buttoned jacket with nothing beneath it but her bra.

Rowie would never have done that. She liked the security of another layer between a jacket and a bra. But Rox had done pretty well at playing her sister today. Surely now she could relax a little. And if these frivolous pink three-inch-spike-heeled pumps—hers, not Rowie's—were a bit over-the-top for a quiet evening, well, she needed the height to keep the trouser hems off the ground and would anyone really be looking at her feet?

Gino apparently had the same idea as she did about relaxing. He heard her coming down the stairs and called to her from the spacious, informal room where she'd eaten her late breakfast this morning. "Rowena?"

"Yes?" She was used to answering to her twin's name, and also to Dr. Madison, which Gino had called her several times today.

He appeared in the doorway. "Would you like something to drink? I was going to give Pia her bath, but Maria asked if she could do it, so…"

He held up a bottle of champagne, which, in hindsight, should have sounded a whole chorus of warning bells, but when had Rox ever listened to that kind of music?

"Champagne would be great," she said.

Gino got a little glint in his eye, which she read incorrectly and grinned back at him. Yeah, he was right, it had been a stressful day. Successful in several areas, but definitely with stresses attached. She still had a niggling fear that Francesco might try to scuttle Rowena's garden design contract as a personal revenge for her rejecting him, even though there was no evidence that he'd talked to Gino about it yet.

It would be nice to unwind a little. Mmm…she could taste those bubbles already.

It was very expensive champagne. It had to be, or else Rox's stomach was emptier than she'd thought, because just half a glass of it went straight to her head and stayed there. Gino put on some music.

Opera.

Tosca.

Sung by Maria Callas and Giuseppe Di Stefano.

Including the part at the end of Act One with the church bells, which she loved and had cried over more than once. As with the champagne bottle warning bells, however, Rox didn't really listen to the bell part of *Tosca* today. She talked to Gino instead.

And even though she couldn't have traced much of a coherent thread in the conversation, she made him laugh and he made her laugh, and just a couple of personal details somehow got themselves dropped into the mix, raising her sense that they were getting to know each other, and that getting to know him felt a lot nicer than she'd expected.

He shared her own appreciation of music and understood the power of drama and emotion in opera. He'd been born to command, so there was a clear-sighted strength to him, and yet she knew he was vulnerable, too, because of Pia. She liked the mix of qualities, liked the way he could surprise her.

In fact…he was really quite cute.

His smile was exceptional, so warm and dark and…*mmm.*

And this was the best champagne she'd ever tasted. Only he was taking it out of her hand. "Wouldn't want you to spill this." A low murmur, husky and sexy and secret, as his dark eyes locked with hers. Yes, the eyes were exceptional, too. She'd noticed them on Pia, but not so much on—

On her shoulder.

His hand was on her shoulder, but it didn't stay there. The warm, soft bulk of his relaxed arm muscles surrounded her. He eased her against his chest, which was still clad in that pristine white Polo shirt that almost glowed against his olive skin. A unique, fabulous scent eddied around her and filled her nostrils—the scent of an Italian man, the scent of Gino. She detected expensive laundry treatments and shower products, coffee and champagne, male skin and male heat.

She still didn't quite believe that this could be happening, or that she could like all of it so much, even though she could feel the press of her breasts against him, tightening as he took a breath. Time kept moving in its usual way. It wasn't supposed to do that in these situations. It was supposed to kind of freeze up at certain points, so that she had the opportunity to think *Gino is going to kiss me.* But it didn't.

The kiss had already happened.

Had *started* happening.

Had started, and wasn't stopping.

Had better not stop any time soon, please, because it was the best kiss she'd had in at least five hundred years. Felt as if it had been that long since anyone had kissed her at all, let alone like this.

Gino tasted like the champagne, and he kissed soft and deep and strong and slow, as if he had all the time in the world, as if this were all he wanted to do. And since right at this moment, it was all Rox wanted to do—all she could imagine *ever* wanting to do—she kissed him back, answering that skilled and gorgeously shaped mouth of his with increasing confidence and heat, gripping Gino wherever her fingers fell.

His body felt fabulous, hard in all the right places. He must find time to work out, because he was built like a discus thrower in an ancient sculpture; only he was made of flesh, not marble, so his muscles were warm and alive. She ran her hands down his back, felt the weight and bulk of his shoulders pressed close to her, realized that they were breathing together. Sheesh, *breathing* together? Yes, she could hear it, feel it, and it seemed so intimate that she was quite shocked.

Low in her body, there was a heaviness, an ache in her belly that focused the pulses from every nerve ending, every sensitized cell in her lips and her fingertips and her nipples. She closed her eyes, because it would be just too overwhelming to keep them open, and it never occurred to her for a second to mistrust anything in what she felt, or anything in what he was doing.

It must have been minutes before they stopped, and stopping was completely Gino's idea. He loosened his delicious hold on her body and stroked a finger from the hollow at the base of her throat down to where the first hint of shadow between her breasts disappeared inside Row's jacket. He brushed her parted lips one last time with his, rested his forehead against hers and whispered, "Don't you wonder what Francesco would think about this?"

Why would Francesco care? I've never met the man!
Oh.
Right.

Gino doesn't know that.

"I—" She stopped.

His eyes had hardened with something like satisfaction, and he read her panicky search for a way out as pure two-timing guilt. "Interesting question, isn't it?" he said.

"You set this whole thing up!" she realized out loud.

"But I hadn't expected it to be so easy."

She was furious now.

And she felt like a fool.

Not that she'd let him guess.

She showed him the anger instead. "You put on one of the most emotional pieces of music ever written, you ply me with champagne on an empty stomach, you laugh at my lame jokes and lower your voice as if you're telling me secrets, then without warning you kiss me so hard and long and deep I can hardly breathe…"

Which had turned out to be a surprisingly good feeling.

Not that she'd let him guess *that,* either.

"…and then you accuse me of being unfaithful toward a man who's openly planning to keep me as his bit on the side after he's married to someone else—"

"Openly?" Gino cut in. "He's said so?"

"Part of today's phone conversation, as it happens. If you've bugged my room, maybe you can get a transcript." She picked up the thread he'd disrupted. "Where I'm from, that's called entrapment, and it's not admissible as evidence in court. But here in your personal autocratic kingdom, I'm already tried, convicted and sentenced on the strength of it, right?"

"I just wanted a little more information as to how you really felt about my brother."

"And this is how you choose to get it. By entrapment."

He shrugged. "It worked."

It hurt!

"Do you have all the information you need now, then?" she asked him sweetly.

"I think so."

"No! You don't!"

"Feel free to give me more."

"Okay, if you're interested—not that you have any right to be, but since you apparently are—I told Francesco on the phone today that I didn't want to get involved with him, and that I wasn't interested in the kind of relationship he was looking for."

"And did he accept that?"

"I don't know."

"You mean he acted as if—"

"I don't know, because I didn't stay on the line to listen. I slammed down the phone. Which was probably my best moment all day."

She picked up her champagne flute, which still had an inch or two of expensive fluid left in the bottom of it. She studied it, then told him, "I'm considering trying to top that moment by pouring this on your head, but on further thought…nah. Why waste it?" She took a final gulp instead and asked, with tinkling politeness, "Could you kindly ask Maria to bring dinner on a tray to my room? Royally ticking off both Di Bartoli brothers in one day turns out to be pretty darned exhausting."

Chapter Four

Something still wasn't right, still didn't gel.

Gino listened to Dr. Madison's echoing heels tap-tapping angrily on the marble floor, getting gradually fainter as she disappeared up the stairs and along the broad corridor to her room. Should he go after her and challenge her? She'd spoken so frankly just now, full of righteous indignation, and yet instinct told him she wasn't telling the whole truth.

His testing of her loyalties seemed to have drastically backfired.

But why did he feel that?

Hadn't he gotten what he wanted?

Twice?

First, she'd returned his carefully engineered kiss with even more enthusiasm and disregard for her supposed feelings for Francesco than he'd expected.

The depth of contact between the two of them had ambushed him like a thief on a Roman backstreet and left him incredibly unsettled.

The impression of life and passion and sexual generosity in the American woman had taken hold of all his senses and wouldn't let go. When had he ever been kissed with such naked enthusiasm? His blood was still beating harder in his veins, and his groin felt heavy with need.

Second, she'd turned out not to have any feelings for Francesco at all, and claimed that any possibility of an affair between them was now over, which should mean that Francesco's future marriage to Marcellina was secure, just as Gino and the Di Bartoli Corporation needed it to be. Dr. Madison had apparently slammed down the phone to emphasize her point. This was a less generous action than her kiss, but just as passionate and life-filled.

The phone.

All right, that should be his next step. Call Francesco himself and check out her story. No slamming required.

For privacy, Gino retreated to his office and got through at once to his younger brother, who confirmed Dr. Madison's account, only with a very different attitude.

"She's completely two-faced, Gino. We should sack her right now. Keeping me dangling for what felt like months with her supposed shyness and virtue and repressed needs. She almost had me fooled!"

"Fooled?" The word gave Gino a prickle of uneasiness.

"I trod so carefully, not wanting to scare her off. And yet today on the phone she's as blunt as a fishwife. It must all have been an act, before. I'm telling you, sack her! She can't treat me like that and get away with it."

"But you can treat her the way you did and get away with it, Francesco?" Gino put in, his tone mild.

"What the hell do you mean?"

"Did you ask her to be your mistress? Or did you promise to end your engagement?"

"Well…both. I tried both."

"And you weren't serious about either."

"She knew that. A woman expects to hear those lines, but she doesn't believe them, Gino. Or she's a fool if she does. Rowena could have done with a lesson or two in the ways of the real world. It was a favor on my part. She was hopelessly naive for a woman of her age, after all those years of being shut away with her ancient garden plans and botanical treatises." He paused for a moment. "Or so she had me believe. But no, it was all an act."

Was it? There was a glaring inconsistency in what Francesco had said about Dr. Madison, but was one side of her apparently split personality an act and the other the real thing? If so, which?

Instinct told Gino it had to be more complicated than that, because there was no way he could identify any obvious fakery in any of it. The timid, bookish woman he'd worked with in earlier meetings and the outspoken, vibrant woman he'd seen—seen, talked to and kissed—over the past twenty-four hours both seemed totally genuine.

Something really wasn't right here.

"I'm glad I spoke to you, Francesco," he told his brother.

"So you're going to deal with her?"

"Yes, I think there are definitely a couple of things that need to be dealt with," Gino agreed.

"Good. I'll look forward to a report."

"You'll get one when there's something to say. Please give my regards to Marcellina. She deserves better."

"Yes?" Francesco laughed, unfazed by the criticism. "Do me a favor, big brother. Keep that opinion to yourself."

Seventeen minutes and twenty seconds.

That was how long Roxanna had to wait before the knock sounded outside her room. Maria with her dinner on a tray?

Oh, please! She had a healthier respect for Gino Di Bartoli's forceful character than that!

She opened the heavy wooden door slowly, annoyed at the feeling of physical weakness that suddenly swept over her. She was sorry that she'd kicked off her heeled shoes. The extra height would have been an advantage right now.

"Yes, Gino?"

There. Nice and cool. Sounding as if the kiss they'd shared had happened in another life.

"Are you going to let me in?"

You mean I have to stop leaning on this lovely heavy oak door and actually support my own weight?

"Yes, if you've come to apologize."

"I've come for that, and for information."

The apology sounded safer. In a clipped, confident voice, Rox asked for it first. Gino had the upper hand, however, and she knew it. Did her fingers usually flutter around her like this? The onslaught of nerves reminded her of the worst scenes she'd had with Harlan, when he was in one of those moods where he would never acknowledge that she could do a single thing right.

Gino moved through the room as if he owned it.

Which, of course, he did.

"I am sorry that I attempted to trap you with a kiss," he said. A beat of silence followed, like a minim rest in a bar of music notation. Rox had time to notice once more how alike Gino and his daughter looked. Dark eyes so steady and deep. Mouth like a smooth, wide bow. "I am even more sorry that, on a purely physical level, we both seem to have enjoyed it."

"Yes, that was tough for me, too," she blurted out. "Not in the plan, for sure."

Their eyes met, shared a flash of alarm and recognition, then skated away from each other again. Rox's insides went tight. Gino took several more prowling paces. He narrowly escaped tripping over her discarded pink shoes, and ended up with his hand on the antique Louis-the-something-or-other writing desk, getting his balance back where it should be. Rox couldn't even look at him.

She hugged her arms around her body as if these prickling goose bumps came from the evening chill. She caught the faintest waft of that masculine scent of his and wanted to chase it, capture it, inhale it in huge lungfuls. Her whole body felt hungry, curious, overwhelmed.

If she had been able to look at Gino, she might have been able to stay one step ahead.

As it was, however…

"Who is Louise Odier?" he suddenly asked, wheeling around and almost impaling her on the sharp point of his question, like a lawyer in a courtroom attacking a witness.

"Louise—? I haven't the faintest idea." Indignant, truthful…disastrous.

His eyes glinted and narrowed. "You have her name

written down right there." He pointed to the piece of paper lying on top of the scattered heap of lists and garden plans.

"Oh my gosh, she's a rose." Again, if Rox had managed to merely think this, instead of blurting it aloud, that might have been more useful to her sister.

Gino picked up the piece of paper and read out with lead weights of emphasis, "'Ask Rowie about Louise Odier!!!' Three exclamation points, Dr. Madison."

"Um, yes, as I said, she's a rose. *Louise Odier* is a type of rose." About which Rox could remember not a single detail and hadn't been able to find reference to in Rowena's notes earlier, which was why she'd written that slapdash memo, reminding herself to check.

"And you are an acknowledged expert on roses, so why would you need to ask?" He stepped closer, as solid and intimidating as a medieval castle wall. "And who would you need to ask?"

"Um—"

"If you wrote this, who is Rowie? Or possibly it's better to ask, who are *you?* Because despite the uncanny resemblance, the woman who kissed me back with such heat just now—" his gaze dropped to her lips, which suddenly felt soft and wouldn't stay pressed together "—is quite definitely *not* the one who outlined her plans for my garden in a meeting several weeks ago, is she?"

Roxanna closed her eyes, seeking an instant infusion of guidance that failed to come. She'd left herself wide-open, gone beyond the point of mending the situation. Time to face reality like the veteran survivor of unsuccessful singing auditions that she was.

Opening her eyes again, she found Gino another two steps closer to where she stood. The intensity of his regard had ratcheted up another notch, and if she hadn't been married to Harlan for so many years, she might have been scared about his intentions. Knowing that there were worse men than the kind who snapped their issues down on the table like a straight line of cards, however, she held her ground and snapped down a few cards of her own.

"She's my twin," she said. "Rowena is my twin."

For a moment, Gino's eyes flared with surprise, but he quickly understood. "Identical?"

"Biologically, yes. But she was much more frail than me at birth, so we're more different than some people expect."

His eyes dropped to her slightly fuller figure, and her personalized stylistic interpretation of Rowena's clothes. "So it would seem. Still, identical enough to trade places when required."

"Especially in the company of people who don't know either of us well."

"Not very professional, such a game. More appropriate for eight-year-olds in a school playground. And you don't share your sister's qualifications in the history of European garden design, do you?"

What does a covert operative do when her cover is irretrievably blown?

Swallowing a cyanide capsule in order to take the secrets of her career in espionage with her to the grave seemed like a slight overreaction, Rox decided. "Where are the darned cyanide capsules when you need them, anyhow?" she muttered under her breath.

Gino frowned, but didn't challenge her to repeat the statement in an audible voice.

"No, and I don't share my sister's crippling anxiety disorder, either," she told him out loud. "This wasn't her fault."

"No? It was yours?"

"It was your brother's, if we have to lay blame."

"Francesco put the two of you up to this? Let's play a trick on my big brother, girls? Something like that?"

She shook her head impatiently, knowing that Gino's misinterpretation was deliberate. Who was playing childish games now?

"Francesco wouldn't leave her alone, Gino," she said. "Rowena isn't used to that kind of European flattery and persistence, and she didn't know how to respond, how to gauge his sincerity or even her own feelings. She reached London and had a serious panic attack at the thought of coming back. She—"

Her voice threatened to crack, but she wouldn't let it. She drew in a breath and went on, while Gino listened.

"She couldn't even leave her hotel room on her own. I've known for several months that she needed treatment, but she wasn't ready to confront that idea herself until now. I agreed to come here to try and carry through the garden project without you or Francesco realizing the substitution, but only on her promise that this time she would get professional help."

"She's still in London?"

"No, my mother flew over there and brought her home to Florida. They're going to look for the right therapist there. Rowena has given me her notes, she's talked about where everything is up to, and we've already been in touch by phone. There's no reason why the project can't continue to run smoothly with me acting as a liaison. She's worked so hard."

Suddenly Roxanna felt close to tears, but she wasn't going to let Gino see them. What would be the point? He would never believe they were genuine.

"Your logic is flawed, Dr.—" He stopped and swore in Italian beneath his breath. "But you don't have a doctorate, do you? And I don't even know your name."

"Roxanna," she told him.

"So, Roxanna, explain why my family was happy to pay the top rate for this sort of work, if your sister's expertise was never necessary, if an unqualified substitute such as yourself can do the job just as well."

"My sister's expertise is necessary, and you'll still have it. You've had all her input so far. On top of that, as I've said, she's given me all her notes, and we can talk by phone as often as we need to. We communicate very well together, as you'd expect. You're not losing out, and you're helping her future."

"Although possibly not her future *clients,* if something like this happens again on her next project at a less convenient stage in the process."

"She's getting treatment." It sounded weak and defensive, but at heart Rox was simply scared.

Yes, Rowena had promised to get treatment, but what if she couldn't find a therapist she trusted? What if she ran away from the whole process halfway through? What if the problem proved to be too deep-seated to cure? How much would it shatter Row's remaining confidence if Rox got her fired from this project before the therapy had even started?

Gino had begun to walk toward the door with a winner's stride.

Let him go?

Not likely. Rox had more fight and stubbornness in her than that.

"I can't ask you to care about my sister," she said. "We tried to trick you, and in hindsight maybe we should have been honest from the beginning." He stopped with his hand poised to turn the handle. "But I can ask you to think about your own interests before you make a decision you might regret."

"I never regret my decisions."

"Just like you never give in to Pia's tantrums, right?"

His face darkened at once.

"Okay, Gino, low blow," she added quickly. "I apologize."

"You don't intimidate easily, do you?"

"No. Not when I know I'm right. Think about how long it would take you to find someone else to oversee this project and get them up to speed on its details. The roses have been ordered. I'm not sure—because you're right, I'm not an expert—how long they can sit around in a shed waiting to go in the ground if the beds aren't fully prepared when they arrive, but I don't imagine their sitting around is a good thing. Rowena would know, and I can ask her. Rowena is on fire about this new concept—"

"Which was her idea? You were her mouthpiece?"

"No, it was mine. And let's not make a big deal out of it. It involved one simple switch in our thinking. But she loves it, and she's going to take it and run with it and come up with something even better. Please don't give me an answer now. In fact, I'm not listening to your answer now." She made a play of pressing her hands to her ears. "Give me a time tomorrow morning when we can meet in your office and I'll hear it then."

Stop now, Rox. Remember Harlan's Reason Number Eleven: "You think that going on and on and on is going to get you what you want, and I guess once in a blue moon it might, but that's purely because you've managed to drive the person nuts with the sheer number of words."

And driving Gino Di Bartoli nuts might not be the best way to go.

He was watching her with the same narrow-eyed intensity he'd shown all through their conversation. She had to bite her lip not to say everything over again, with even more emphasis and pleading and logic.

"Tomorrow at ten," he finally said. Then he looked around the room, his face like a mask. "If you haven't unpacked yet, I suggest you don't. Not until after we've talked in the morning." He looked at his watch. "Meanwhile, Maria will be up with your dinner tray soon."

"I'll—" She stopped.

Go stir-crazy if I have to eat in my room after this little scene.

"Yes?"

"Look forward to it," she improvised instead.

What was I going to do, anyhow, she wondered, *beg to be let out?*

"Tomorrow," he repeated, and a few seconds later he had gone.

His departure left Rox with the realization that she really would go stir crazy if she had to eat in her room and then spend half the night here fighting her jet lag and trying to get to sleep, with her sister's professional and emotional future hanging in the balance. She prowled around for a few minutes, then sat in the padded wooden window seat and looked restlessly out at the view, like Rapunzel in her tower waiting for her hair to grow.

Finally, she decided that the only thing to do was get down to Maria before Maria got up here to her. She wasn't proud. She'd eat in the kitchen. Since Gino probably never set foot there, he wouldn't find out.

And Maria might have some inside information on the way to her lordship's…uh, correction…her *boss's* heart—no reason to get too medieval with her terminology here—because on that point, Harlan was right. She was persistent when it really counted. If she got a *no* at ten o'clock tomorrow morning, Rox fully intended to keep on arguing.

Rowena's career was too important—it was the only thing she had.

Sneaking down the back stairs like Cinderella ignoring her stepsisters' floor-scrubbing orders, Rox located Maria's kitchen by means of its heavenly smell. Better than anything that wafted from a New York pizza restaurant, she decided.

The older woman was just setting a plate of pasta on a tray, along with two bread rolls in a little basket and a side-dish of buttered asparagus. Gino and his daughter must already have their own plates in front of them in the formal dining room.

"Hi, Maria," Rox said quickly. "No need for that tray, I'm here."

"You're not to eat in your room? You are eating with Signor Di Bartoli and Meess Pia?" She gestured in the direction of the dining room, from which Rox could just hear faint voices, one deep and one high, like a duet for cello and piccolo.

"No, no," she said. "I'll eat here. If that's okay. Please."

"Here?"

"I don't want to make a fuss, Maria. I'm tired, and I'm sure you are, too, and for either of us to take that tray all the way upstairs when I can just sit here, it doesn't make sense."

Maria threw up her hands. "It's for you to say, Dr. Madison. You are a guest. You eat where you wish."

So Gino hadn't told Maria yet that Rox wasn't quite the guest that the Di Bartoli family wanted.

"And you'll eat with me, won't you?" She could see a second pasta plate on the kitchen bench, beside an old-fashioned metal colander and a heavy-bottomed pot containing a meaty sauce that smelled rich with wine and herbs.

"I can wait," Maria said. "You go ahead." Her English was accented and occasionally flawed, but confident.

"Please," Rox begged again. "It's no fun eating alone. We can talk. I can practice my Italian. What's in this sauce? It smells like heaven. Is it a family recipe?"

Bingo!

One look at Maria's face told Rox she'd found the way to the older woman's heart. Hearing about the fresh sage and oregano that had begun its spring growth in the kitchen garden, she watched Maria heap pasta and sauce into the second plate, add more rolls to the basket and place them and the asparagus in the middle of the old wooden table centered in the high-ceilinged room. They both sat down and picked up their forks.

The Pia piccolo in the dining room overrode the Gino cello and launched into a solo, trilling and emphatic. The percussion section of the orchestra got involved for a couple of bars. Fork and plate sounded like triangle and cymbals. A chair gave a scrape and a crash, followed by the rhythm of running feet.

Pia arrived in the kitchen, stormy-faced. She climbed onto a chair, reached into the middle of the table and took a roll from the basket. Didn't say a word. Her father appeared just as she took her first bite, and two identical pairs of dark Di Bartoli eyes glared at each other. Maria and Rox both put their forks quietly into their dishes and waited.

Gino looked around. At the evening sky visible through the windows. At the steam rising from the plates. At the grouping of three females at the table. At the cooking dishes awaiting attention in the huge enameled sinks.

It was a gorgeous kitchen, Rox thought. From the ceiling hung braided strings of onions and garlic bulbs still left from last summer's harvest, as well as bunches of drying herbs. Three ancient, rock-solid wooden dressers housed rows of chunky ceramic dishes and jars of tomatoes and peppers. An enormous wood-burning cast-iron range dominated one end of the room, but she guessed it wasn't often used now. Maybe for heating on winter's coldest days, or for cooking homemade bread and pizza.

A wood fire would make the room even cozier, but it was wonderfully cozy already, with a lived-in imperfection about it that told you it was the heart of the house, not merely a staged scene for a lifestyle magazine article on Tuscan living. The stone-flagged floor was uneven, so two of the table legs had wads of folded paper wedged beneath them, and there was a circular scorch mark on the tabletop near Rox's elbow where someone had once placed a burning-hot pan. Maybe yesterday, maybe a hundred years ago.

For at least two centuries, Di Bartoli servants and family members must have shared gossip here, sneaked in here for treats and tastes between meal times, hidden here alone or in couples to cry or yell or kiss. The polished perfection of the recently redecorated dining room just didn't have the same aura of warmth and history, and its oval table was such a vast expanse that Pia probably felt as if her father were eating his meal on the far side of the moon.

The little girl took another mouthful of her bread roll. It was so crusty that it broke in her mouth with an audible crunch. Her eyes were wide and they didn't move from her papa's face. They'd lost their defiance now. She was simply waiting for his verdict on her behavior, and Rox had the oddest sense that both father and daughter were on trial at this moment. She couldn't help watching Gino's face, also, and she probably wore almost the same beseeching, wary, ready-to-defy look that Pia did.

"Okay," Gino finally said. "We will *all* eat in the kitchen tonight."

Maria jumped up at once. Was that a secret smile of approval? She reached the kitchen door with her back to them all before Rox could get a better look and make up her mind. She stood up herself and said, "Sit down, Gino, while I help Maria bring everything in."

Pia wanted to help, too, and Gino apparently didn't

want to be left sitting at the table on his own, so within a minute or two everything had been brought in and set haphazardly down.

"Bring the cheese now, Maria, then no-one has to get up again," Gino said, and a cheese board and knife and an oval-shaped *marzolino* also appeared on the table.

It was so much nicer than eating in the cold formality of the dining room. Rox accepted half a glass of the red wine that Gino offered, but made only a token attempt to drink it. The champagne had proved to be so dangerous earlier.

Pia finished eating first, but was then happy to sit on the floor attempting to braid the last remaining heads of the previous fall's garlic harvest out of the basketful that Maria gave her, using their dried-out, twinelike leaves. Meanwhile, the adults sat over their bread and cheese, then drank coffee accompanied by some exquisite little chocolates.

Pia managed to find space in her stomach for two of those, of course. She was having trouble with her garlic braiding technique, though. It was going to end up an unsatisfying mess.

Rox had never braided garlic before, but she could see how it should be done. Without stopping to think about issues of dignity—to quote Harlan, and Reason Number Fifteen, "You're not dignified"—she scrambled off her chair, got down to Pia's level and knelt on the floor.

"It's a pattern, Pia, see?" she said. "This side to the middle, other side to the middle, this side to the middle, other side to the middle. Say it like a chant and you won't forget."

"This side to the middle, other side to the middle," Pia repeated, intent and patient and slow.

She'd gotten it beautifully now—she had excellent fine motor control for her age, and was such a quick learner—but she hadn't remembered to add in a new garlic head, so Rox helped her with that and they added it to the pattern of their chant. "This side to the middle, other side to the middle, new head. This side to the middle, other side to the middle…"

Maria and Gino had been talking housekeeping details at first, and Rox didn't realize they'd fallen silent or that Maria was watching the whole process until she heard the housekeeper say in Italian, "That's long enough now, Pia. Don't add any more heads, darling. There are only the smallest ones left, barely worth keeping. Just finish the braid. That will hang just right with the others."

"Good work, Pia," Gino said, which was when Rox realized he'd been watching the process, too. Only he wasn't looking at Pia as he said it; he was looking at her.

Maria cleared most of the dishes from the table, then took Pia's garlic braid, finished it off with some kind of knot that Rox didn't know, and hung it on a spare hook next to the others. "See?"

Pia clapped her hands. "See what I made, Daddy?"

"It's perfect, Pia. Well done, sweetheart."

"Pia, let's go upstairs for your bath now," Maria said, and the little girl took the housekeeper's hand and went off without the slightest protest, still beaming and pleased with herself.

A little flushed, and with a pair of cold and uncomfortable knees from kneeling on the stone floor in only the thin fabric of Row's black trousers, Rox slid back into her chair and finished her last mouthful of coffee and half a chocolate. She tried not to look at Gino, but…was he still watching her?

"You'd make a very good teacher," he said, pouring himself more coffee and cutting another sliver of the strongly flavored cheese.

"Me?" Rox was startled. "Oh, I don't have the patience. Really, I don't."

He took a mouthful of coffee. "You haven't thought about it."

"Trust me, I have! I have a music teaching degree. It was supposed to be my fallback position if the singing career didn't work out, but—"

"So that's what you really do?" He almost smiled his gorgeous smile, but then it faded. Rox felt tempted to stretch across the table and curve the corners of his mouth back up again with her thumbs. *Please smile for me, Gino.* "You're a singer."

"I'm a waitress who wants to be a singer but probably never will be," Rox corrected bluntly.

She lifted her chin and felt the flush on her cheeks get hotter. After lying to Gino about so much over the past day and a half, she'd now been seized by an attack of zealous honesty and wasn't going to lie to herself, either.

She had a nice singing voice and a nice stage presence, yes, but she didn't have that indefinable star quality, that magic pulling power, that operatic strength of projection, and her voice was no better than a thousand others. Dozens of failed auditions had hammered the point home.

"With a music teaching degree," Gino repeated, as if that were way more important than the singing. He had

Pia's intentness in his gaze and Pia's stubbornness. For some reason, he did actually want to talk about this.

"You should have seen me in my practical teaching block," she told him. "Twenty-five children squawking away on their plastic descant recorders. It physically hurt my ears. It hurt my heart. If they weren't tone-deaf, they were acting out in the back row, rude and ratty and unpleasant. And if they weren't doing that, then their fingers wouldn't stretch to the right holes."

Gino nodded, but didn't speak. He put his coffee cup down and leaned closer, one strong brown forearm resting on the table. This table wasn't like the polished rosewood ice-skating rink in the dining room, but it was a still big table. Rox would need to lean closer, also, if they wanted to touch. Not likely, after the scary strength of their earlier kiss, she decided.

"And if they weren't acting out, or tone-deaf, or with the wrong fingers," she went on, "they were just…not interested. Wanted to talk about TV shows instead. And I tried."

"Yes, I can imagine you did."

Hmm, that almost sounded like a compliment.

"But bad recorder playing is so, oh, *ugly,* and it wasn't a wealthy school district and recorders are the cheapest instrument around, so I was told it had to be recorders. And maybe I could have gotten through to some of the kids if I'd had more time, more individual attention to give, but I didn't, and anyhow the minuscule secretions produced by my vestigial patience gland had already run dry and—"

"There are other ways to teach," Gino cut in. "Other kinds of children. Gifted children."

"Pia is very gifted, I think."

She'd tried to tell him this yesterday, and he hadn't been convinced, but the atmosphere between the two of them seemed better now. For Pia's sake, she was prepared to revive the argument. She sat a little straighter in her chair, then leaned forward the way Gino was doing. People naturally did that when they wanted to give an argument more force. They could have touched, now, but they didn't.

"Gifted in music?" He still looked skeptical. "Surely it's too soon to tell."

"Gifted in all sorts of areas. But yes, I think she has a great sense for music and I don't think it's too soon to tell. I used music today, did you notice, when she was having trouble getting the garlic braiding right?"

"I am surprised you are calling it music. I would have said it was a question of her fine motor skills."

"Yes, and Pia's fine motor skills are excellent, but she needed to understand the pattern, too, and she understood it through the rhythm. I mean, rhythm is just pattern for the ears, and if a child learns easiest through rhythm and pattern, then—"

"You see? You should teach music to gifted children," he repeated. "Perhaps one-on-one, or in small groups. You would be very good at it. I, for one, would send Pia to you, since you tell me she has musical talent."

"You would?"

"Yes, why not? I may not be willing to employ you as a garden designer—although you may think it strange," he said mildly, "that I should be so insistent on actual qualifications in the field—"

Yeah. Touché. Did she have the slightest chance of convincing him tomorrow?

"—but as a teacher, where you are not only qualified but gifted with the right…"

He hesitated, searching for a word.

"Skills?" she suggested. Regarding the garden design thing, she clung desperately to the word *may*. "*May* not be willing."

Don't antagonize him at this point, Rox. Listen to what he's telling you. Pretend to be convinced, even if you're not.

Yes, lie to him again.

The kitchen felt too intimate a setting for lies, however, with its shadowy corners and the lingering fragrances of the meal and the worn surface of this table across which they could almost touch but would need to stand and stretch over if they wanted to kiss…

Don't think about that, Rox.

She hoped she wouldn't have to lie. It would really be so much nicer to win on—on—something else. Connection. Or simple respect.

"Skills, but that's only part of it," Gino said, nodding. "Perceptions. Instincts. Imagination. Energy."

"But no patience."

"You would not need patience if you were working with gifted children. You would need to go as fast as you could to keep up with them."

"Mmm," Rox said. She thought for a moment, then said it again. "Mmm. Thank you, I'll…I'll—"

"Think about it."

"Yes, I will."

And in her room, lying awake for half the night, Rox did.

She thought about music teaching, and failed auditions, and all the ways Harlan used to put her down. She thought about Pia's garlic braid and the sense of family history in the old kitchen. She thought about the shape and color and texture of Gino Di Bartoli's bare forearm resting on the kitchen table and the champagne-perfect taste of his mouth during that tricky, unforgivable, fabulous kiss.

And once again, she didn't get to sleep until four.

Chapter Five

It was two minutes till ten o'clock.

In other words, Roxanna Madison had two more minutes, and then she would be late. Gino found himself hoping that she would be. Very late. Forty minutes or more. That would give him the excuse he needed to fire her and her sister without his feeling as if he'd somehow been petty or narrow in vision.

He felt stuck.

Torn.

Suspicious of his own motives.

He wasn't accustomed to any of those feelings in relation to women or to employees. Sitting back in his chair, he anchored his heels on the floor and swiveled to and fro, looking at the view from his office window, of sky and vineyard and distant hills, and listening to the sounds of daily activity that penetrated his private space.

A door banged shut. He heard a male voice—one of the gardeners greeting Maria. Water ran, making a faint thumping sound in the pipes. Was Roxanna in the shower? Was that her weight making an old floorboard creak upstairs? What should he do about her?

"Where has my judgment gone?" he muttered to himself in Italian.

Normally, he found hiring and firing easy. The family corporation went after the best people and offered them the kind of money and working environment that meant that they stayed and they performed to expectations. If they proved unsatisfactory, which didn't often happen, they were told why and they were let go, usually with generous severance.

As for women…

All the girlfriends he'd had before marriage had been a precise fit with his circumstances at the time. During his studies, he'd dated a couple of wild partygoers, as well as an intense and brilliant philosophy student. In his first couple of years with Di Bartoli, he'd chosen junior female executives working for companies who had a professional relationship with his own corporation—in advertising, for example.

When he'd met Angele, she'd had Marriage Material written all over her. No evidence of the wrong men in her past, the right social ambitions and not too many professional ones. At twenty-seven, Gino had felt quite smug about his impeccable judgment.

But then the marriage hadn't worked.

And the fact that it wasn't working had been so obvious to both of them that, once again, their divorce had seemed like a piece of strong strategic action on

Gino's part. The right response to a new situation. The right change of tack.

But maybe he had been wrong about that. Maybe all he'd done in divorcing Angele was to undo a mistake he never should have made in the first place.

A discreet tap sounded at his office door. His watch read exactly ten o'clock.

"Come in," he called, his decision about the future of the Madison garden contract still unmade.

Three seconds later, the uncertainty had disappeared.

Because Roxanna had Pia with her. *Attached* to her, in fact. Pia was sitting on a sneaker-clad foot with her arms and legs wrapped around one very shapely right calf covered in khaki cotton.

"Sorry," Roxanna told him cheerfully. "I have something stuck to my foot and it won't come off. I noticed a mud scraper out by the back door. Do you think that might work?"

Pia giggled and gurgled and grinned, and Roxanna was so clearly enjoying herself just as much as his daughter that Gino didn't have the heart to come down hard on either of them. Pia needed moments like this in her life. Maybe she needed a woman like this…

"It might," he agreed, talking about the mud scraper. "Or could I suggest a pair of tweezers? A crowbar? Or Maria might have some kind of stain remover in her laundry room. It does look like a very nasty kind of spot, I must say."

Pia thought his humor was hysterical, and it felt so good to have made her laugh instead of yell and scream and tighten her face with that thunderous frown of hers that, no, really, he just couldn't ruin the mood by taking a harsh line on the Madison sisters' deception.

Rox pretended to use tweezers, crowbar and stain remover, and finally Pia was declared to have "miraculously vanished." She went along with the idea, still giggling, and nodded and ran off when Rox told her, "Meet you outside soon?"

Pia closed the door, leaving the two of them alone together as the squeak of her rubber-soled shoes faded. Then Rox looked Gino straight in the eye and asked, bold as brass, "So? Am I permitted to unpack now?" A second later, Rox screwed up her face a little and added in a much smaller voice, "Please?"

Gino schooled his own expression into a look that was much more stern than the way he actually felt. He could still hear Pia's laughter in his memory, and it warmed something inside him that he'd forgotten was even there. "Your manners and your begging face won't get you anywhere at this point," he said. "My decision is already made."

Roxanna took his curt tone without flinching and nodded. "Yes, of course. I understand."

"I will keep you on here to see the project through to completion. I will also ask that in return you spend some time with Pia when you can."

"Oh! Oh, thank you! Yes, of course I can spend time with Pia. I'd love to."

"If I'm happy at that point, your sister will get her glowing reference and the new lines on her résumé. If I'm not happy, you may wish you'd chosen to leave now."

Rox was too relieved to be impressed by the threat,

which she waved away, her cheeks flushing at the same time.

"You'll be happy," she promised. "Rowie is so excited about this. I heard from her late last night. She's already written some draft text for the information plaques she wants to mount beside each antique rose."

"I'll look forward to examining her concept for those in more detail," Gino said, careful not to take on any of Roxanna's glowing enthusiasm, which was surprisingly hard to resist.

"She can e-mail it to you for your approval whenever you want. She also had some suggestions for the gardeners this morning. I'll go out and see them now, if there's nothing you need me for in the house."

"No, I don't need you. I'm busy all morning."

Now there was an unmistakable dismissal, Rox thought as she left the house.

Gino Di Bartoli was an arrogant man, accustomed to obedience and control. He'd made it clear that she was only still here on his whim, and that she and her sister had better perform accordingly.

Which was fair, when you thought about it.

Rox did think about it. It stayed in the back of her mind all day while she supervised the gardeners, entertained Pia and gave her another impromptu piano lesson. And it still hovered in the back of her mind in the kitchen at five o'clock as she developed a major conspiracy with Maria, over a glass of iced juice, regarding where everyone would eat their meals from now on.

The conspiracy took a while to get right.

"Signora Angele believed that children need to learn

how to eat a proper meal with good table manners, Dr. Madison," Maria said, "and I know that Signor Gino agreed with her."

"And I agree with her, too," Rox said, "but surely that doesn't mean Pia has to eat a three-course meal in that enormous dining room three times every day? Does it mean I have to eat in that enormous dining room three times every day? It slows down breakfast and lunch when I want to get outside."

She'd worked hard today and so had the gardeners, but according to Rowena's rough daily schedule, they were a little behind, because the gardeners had been waiting for Rox's next set of instructions while she was still demonstrating good table manners at lunch.

"There is the sunroom where the family sometimes eats, especially in the summer," Maria said, "but Signor Gino has given that to you as your office, so he has said it can't be used for meals."

"Oh, but that's not necessary. It's ridiculous!"

Well, maybe not so ridiculous, Rox mentally revised, thinking of how the room looked at the moment.

A mess. No room for serving dishes and plates, or even human backsides on chairs.

She'd barely spent any time in it, but she'd visited it several times today to leaf hastily through Rowie's books and notes and catalogues in search of something her sister had talked about on the phone or mentioned in the notes she'd written in London.

Hasty leafing was not a tidy process. The round wrought iron table was covered in papers and piles of books, as were the chairs and the bookshelves. She'd moved the computer to the sideboard, because when she came in from the garden to check a file on screen, it was easier to do it standing up.

"I don't need a separate office," she told Maria. "My bedroom is huge. It would actually be more convenient to move everything up there, because now that I'm consulting with my—" She stopped.

Better remember to keep her conspiracies straight. So far, only Gino knew that she wasn't her sister, the real garden expert.

"Because I sometimes like to work at night or in the early morning," she said instead, "and I wouldn't want to disturb anyone by coming downstairs at odd hours."

"The sunroom is much better," Maria agreed. "Closer to the kitchen. Easier for me. We could open the French doors when the weather gets warm and have picnic lunches on the terrace. Pia could have another child to dinner, since it is more relaxed. The family's local doctor has a nice little girl. You're right, Dr. Madison. We can arrange things. This fuss over the little one's tantrums, when all she really needs is…" She sighed, clucked her tongue and shook her head.

Rox nodded sympathetically. No discussion required. They were in complete agreement regarding how *not* to raise a gifted child. "Let me clear out that room right away, Maria," she said, determined to have the job done in time for tonight's meal.

Maria nodded. "I will help."

And Rox knew it was a signal of approval as much as an offer of assistance. Later that night, she unpacked the rest of her own things and used the emptied suitcase to store the clothes of Rowena's that she knew she wouldn't use.

She was staying at the *Palazzo Di Bartoli*, and she was going to make it work.

Spring had really arrived now.

Gino could smell it in the air, see it in the light and hear it in the chirping of the birds, but even if he'd been without most of his senses, he would still have felt the change of season stirring his blood. He sat at his desk, stiff in the spine from having worked since six this morning without taking a break. He'd even eaten breakfast in here today.

Standing, he went to the window and did some stretches, the fabric of his black T-shirt and old jeans giving easily with the movement. It was nearly eleven, and he'd barely been aware of the activity around the place because he'd spent most of the morning on the phone.

He had been here at the *palazzo* with Pia and Roxanna for just over two weeks, which was strange because it didn't feel like that length of time. At certain moments, it felt like the blink of an eye, while at others it could have been at least two months.

His daily timetable had fallen into a rough rhythm that he liked. Pia was an early riser, so he got up with her at six, and at that time of day she would happily "work" alongside him in his office for a good hour and a half, drawing and cutting out magazine pictures without more than a sentence or two of interruption. He hadn't confessed to anyone how much he was beginning to enjoy these quiet sessions together.

At around seven-thirty, they'd eat breakfast and then he'd hand her over to Maria or Roxanna for the morning. He'd see her at lunch and then not again until around five, when he'd usually emerge from his office and hear the piano. Pia had a music lesson almost every day. He liked to listen to it but didn't want Roxanna or Pia to know he was doing so, which meant he skulked just outside the door and only stayed for a few minutes.

They ate most of their meals in the sunroom now, and if they didn't eat in the sunroom, they ate in the kitchen. Maria had managed to communicate that it lightened her workload that way, and since she had so much more on her daily agenda with Pia in the house, he hadn't argued, even though he suspected Roxanna's covert involvement in making the change.

To be honest, mealtimes were far more relaxed as a result and he was relieved, despite the niggling awareness in the back of his mind that certain people might have thought he'd started "giving in" to his housekeeper and his garden consultant now, as well as to his daughter.

The evening meal was his favorite. It reminded him of summer evenings in his childhood when cousins or family friends would visit, housekeeping staff would have the night off, and no-one could be bothered with formality. His mother and her sisters or her friends would prepare huge bowls of pasta or salad or the bean dishes which Tuscans traditionally loved, and everyone would gather in the kitchen to help, or they'd all sit at the long table outside, beneath the grape arbor, talking over their food for hours.

What had happened to that table? He couldn't remember. He remembered the deaths of his parents, however, as if they'd happened yesterday. His father had had a stroke in his early fifties, while his mother had been diagnosed with cancer just two years later. They'd never even known Angele, let alone Pia. Time had softened the sense of loss, and now he mainly remembered his mother's magnetic, emotional personality, the tangled threads of endless conversation, and just the sheer pleasure everyone took in each other's company.

Those kinds of evenings didn't happen often enough now, but somehow he recaptured a little of their essence in his zesty mealtime conversations with Roxanna.

And if he sometimes suspected that she deliberately avoided too much time in his company, especially when they were alone…well…it saved him from reliving the ill-advised kiss he'd tried to trick her with two weeks ago, so he should be grateful for her strategy.

He was grateful to her for other reasons.

Pia hadn't had a tantrum since last Thursday evening. Almost a week.

And she had a little friend! She'd spent two afternoons with the doctor's daughter, five-year-old Ciara, and Ciara was coming here to play next Monday. Thinking about the other little girl, Gino realized he didn't know the names of any of Pia's friends in Rome.

Surely…

No, he couldn't think of one.

On an impulse, he called his sister-in-law. "Tell me the names of Pia's friends, Lisette."

"Off the top of my head, my dear Gino?" Her Italian was almost perfect, as was her English. Angele's and Lisette's mother had been American by birth.

"Is it that hard?" he asked.

"Well… Are you planning a party for her? If you want a comprehensive list, Miss Cassidy will have one, with their addresses, but I can tell you a few."

"Please do."

"There are the Von Dorffs. A very good family. He is a wine expert, supposedly, but of course their money is very old. The wine is only a hobby. They have two boys, Klaus and Emil, aged, oh, around eight and ten. And the Borgheses. The younger branch of the family. They have a girl, Anna. She's about fourteen months old, very pretty, with blond—"

"Pia's friends, Lisette," he cut in. "Not families whose children we can invite to formal parties."

"But it's the same thing!"

"She can't really be friends with toddlers or boys twice her age."

"People aren't having so many children, you see. You have no idea, Gino! It's sometimes impossible to find good, top-drawer families with the right match of age and gender. Miss Cassidy does very well encouraging Anna and Pia to play together. Would you like me to fax you the list?"

"No, don't bother."

He talked with Lisette for a little longer, but it wasn't satisfying since she couldn't help him with Pia's friends. In fact, he didn't hear half of what she said, because the gardeners had come around to work on this side of the house and he could hear Roxanna and Pia instead. When he'd put down the phone, he gave up any pretense of more work for the moment and just listened.

There must be a game of hide-and-seek in progress. It was one of Pia's favorites. Oh, now she had apparently fetched her drawing supplies and was making a picture. Hmm, and next a piggyback ride, which lasted for a heroic length of time while Roxanna instructed the gardeners and came back into the house and up to her room to check some notes.

"Can horsies climb stairs?" he heard, in a little voice that echoed like a bell against the stone floors of the old *palazzo*.

"Clever ones can."

"Why is it called a piggyback if you're a horse?"

"I don't know. It should be called a horseyback, shouldn't it? Can you make the clip-clop sound with your tongue now, Pia? My tongue's getting tired. Do you hear the rhythm of it? We'll play that same rhythm on the piano later on, when we have our lesson."

Gino looked at the report on his desk, slated as the next item needing attention. It summarized the results of consumer testing on a new Di Bartoli moisturizer. He tried to make sense of it, but the focus group quotes were the usual riddles of inconsistency. Loved the fragrance. Hated the fragrance. Loved the packaging. Couldn't get the lid open. Loved the name. Didn't know how the name should be pronounced.

His eyes blurred and the words started to look like musical notes dancing along the lines. A mouthful of cold coffee didn't help. It was almost lunchtime. He felt restless, and the phone conversation with Lisette had left a sour taste in his mouth for some reason. He wanted to do something reckless and impulsive to get rid of it and change his mood.

He decided that he needed to stretch his legs out in the fresh spring air, where he should also check on the progress of the garden, because he should still be careful not to let the nondoctor Madison twin think she'd won any final victories yet. The final payment on her sister's contract was due on completion, and there was work still to be done.

He saw her as soon as he stepped down from the terrace. The gardeners had already stopped work for their lunch break, and Pia must have come inside the house to Maria. Roxanna wandered around in the sunshine, checking details of her sister's plan against what the gardeners had done this morning. Many of the roses were now planted, and she was making sure the labels attached to the thorny canes matched the names on Rowena's design.

She hadn't seen Gino yet, and he took shameless advantage of the fact. He wanted to study her when she wasn't aware of him, because he really needed to work her out.

No.

Work himself out.

What was this attraction all about? After two weeks…fifteen days, really…it hadn't gone away, it had only gotten stronger. And it made the air between them so thick in the rare moments when they found themselves alone together that he wasn't at all surprised about how carefully Roxanna avoided such moments.

She wore a pair of khaki pants that were filthy with dark brown dirt at the knees as if she'd been kneeling on the bare ground. They were streaked with the same dirt on her backside, where she'd obviously been wiping her hands. He could just imagine what those must look like if she hadn't been wearing gloves.

She definitely hadn't been wearing gloves. He found them casually tossed next to a potted kumquat tree and picked them up to bring them to her. She saw him as he came toward her, holding them out.

"Oh, thanks, they've been lost all morning. Where did you find them?" She stood silhouetted against the old garden wall, whose pitted stones had a warm yellow glow in the sunshine, and she'd forgotten to push her sunglasses down. They sat on the top of her head, while she had to narrow her eyes against the midday brightness.

"Flung on the ground behind one of the citrus tubs," he told her. She took them…and immediately flung them down again, into the empty wheelbarrow that sat at the edge of the garden bed.

"Bit late for them now." She showed him her hands, laughing and grimacing.

They were appalling, stiff with dried dirt, their nails outlined by the mud that had filled the groove around each cuticle. She could scrub for ten minutes and her hands would still be stained. There was a streak of dirt along her jawline, also. If she knew about it, she didn't care.

"Couldn't the gardeners have lent you a pair?" Gino suggested.

She turned her mouth upside down, rejecting the idea. "Their gloves are just as dirty inside as they are on the outside. I hate gloves, anyhow. You can't feel what you're doing."

"What were you doing?"

"Checking the depth of the holes. Poking around. I thought I'd found an archaeological site." She grinned suddenly, and her tone turned a little self-mocking. "I had visions of Roman jewels and coins and pottery shards, but it was just a piece of bone and a tin can." She'd obviously enjoyed the naive thrill of discovery while it had lasted and didn't mind poking fun at herself about her disappointment.

"Bad luck." He stepped closer. Hadn't intended to, but couldn't stay away. He'd spent too much time thinking about her this morning.

"You're laughing at me." She leaned back and tilted her head to one side, pressing her shoulder blades against the rough stone of the wall and crossing one sock-clad ankle over the other. The pose pushed her hips and breasts forward in a way that looked relaxed and teasing at the same time.

"You like making me laugh at you," Gino said.

This time, Roxanna was the one who laughed, clearly intrigued by his statement. "Now how in the world have you managed to work that out after just a couple of weeks?" she murmured.

"So it's true?" He knew it was. And he liked being right about her.

"Um, yes." She scraped her teeth across her bottom lip, parodying a child's expression of apology.

"You're not very good at hiding what you think and feel, Roxanna." She'd expressed various strong opinions and strong emotions over their mealtime conversations. They'd had some lively arguments together.

They looked at each other, and he wanted to kiss her so much that he could hardly breathe. Why not? Why the hell not kiss her, when they were both free and reasonable adults? Lisette had dropped several hints lately about him finding an outlet for his male needs. A few weeks ago, Francesco hadn't hesitated when it came to seducing Roxanna's far more vulnerable sister, and Gino wasn't encumbered by another involvement as his brother was.

His eyes dropped to her mouth. No dirt there. No

makeup, either. Just a beautiful bow of soft, sensitive pink that parted at its seam on an uneven inbreath when she saw what he was looking at. Her eyes softened and went wide. She pushed herself off the wall and stood upright again.

But she was waiting for him, not preparing to run away.

The impulse to kiss her grew even stronger now that Gino knew she wanted it just as much. His decision wasn't made, it just…happened. A few seconds later, as he stepped closer, she began to laugh again, with that teasing, challenging glint back even stronger in her incredible blue eyes.

"Would you really, Gino, when I'm this filthy?" she asked him softly.

"I think I can find ways around that problem."

He took a final step and reached for her wrists, circling his thumb and middle finger around each of them and lifting those dirt-caked hands safely out of the way. He tipped her back against the wall and widened his stance so that his legs bracketed hers. Not wanting to hurt her, he rested the backs of his own hands against the roughness of the stone and didn't care about the way it ground into his skin.

"You're inventive…very lateral," she whispered.

"And that's good?"

"Yes." She was still watching his lips, watching the way they moved when he spoke.

"Thank you," he said. "A compliment."

"You're welcome, Gino."

Before he even touched her mouth, the moment was way more intimate than their entire first kiss had been. They watched each other, silent and expectant, teasing each other with waiting. Gino hadn't known that a woman's eyes so intently fixed on his mouth could be so erotic…especially when she so clearly knew what she was doing to him, and what she was going to do to that mouth very soon.

They were both vulnerable like this. Neither had the upper hand. He had her pinned here, but she could twist away from him any time she wanted, and she would throw him off balance if she did. He could feel the heat of her core, the hardness of her hips, the firm push of her breasts, the unsteady way she breathed.

He wanted her so much!

Why had he wasted so many days pretending he didn't?

When his mouth closed over hers, she made a little cry—need and satisfaction, tangled together. She tried to move her hands to touch him, but he wouldn't let her, so she had to caress him with her body instead. And that felt…

There were no words.

She slid her hips from side to side like a belly dancer, arched her back and pushed her breasts harder against his body. Her breathing got faster, matching his. His mouth left hers and trailed down, briefly tasting metallic clay as he crossed her jaw. He tasted the natural sweetness of her skin once more as he covered her throat and reached the neckline of her T-shirt, right at the center where the fabric parted below a single unfastened pearly button.

He buried his face between her breasts and she gasped. That was when he let go of her hands. She took advantage of the freedom at once and must have forgotten all about the dirt. She took his face between those mud-roughened palms, scooped his head up so she could kiss him again, ravished his mouth with open hunger.

And I don't care about the dirt, he thought hazily. *I'd roll naked with her in a patch of mud like a pig and I'd laugh about it. This is so different. This is not me, is it?*

The sour taste of his conversation with Lisette had definitely gone, replaced by…*dirt?*

He knew the moment Roxanna remembered her hands, because she pulled back so fast that she almost took him with her, and then she shrieked.

"Look what I've done! I've made a complete mess of you."

He just grinned. "I have a beard now?"

"Sideburns better than Elvis ever managed. I'm sorry." She smirked at him and made a helpless gesture.

"You're not sorry at all."

"Well, I am, but it's pretty funny, too. Like the dye they put with banknotes that gets triggered if there's a robbery. We'll be caught red-handed if we can't get this to wash off…" She frowned and stroked her fingers across his jaw again, taking her own words seriously only after she'd spoken them.

"Surely that's making it worse," he murmured.

"Hmm, yes, correct again, Sherlock. Let's see… A hose?" She looked around.

"I don't care, Roxanna."

"I think a hose would be better than a watering can."

"I don't care if you can't get it off."

"Maria will—"

"Something is happening here," he said, very deliberately. He'd captured her attention now. She let go of her scatty quest for a water source and locked her gaze onto his. "It's been building between us for two weeks. Why should I want to hide it from Maria?"

"Why—" She shook her head.

He'd startled her, pulled the ground from under her feet. He could see it in the way her shoulders stiffened and hunched, and in the way she wrapped her arms around each other and held them protectively across her body.

Why hadn't she expected him to speak openly about what had just happened? Why hadn't she known that he would want to take it further? They were adults, answerable to no-one but themselves and a handful of people they cared about.

"I—It was just a kiss, Gino," she said.

"No, it wasn't." He stepped close to her again. "There's no such thing as just a kiss."

"No?"

"When it's a bad kiss, no-one wants a repetition. When it's a good kiss—a fabulous kiss—then I want more. Don't you? We've wasted two weeks on preten—"

"So you jump into bed with every woman who knows how to kiss?"

"Of course I don't."

"It sure sounds that way."

"You think so many women know how to kiss?"

"I don't think I'm anything special in that area. I know I'm not."

"What would be your definition of special?" he asked.

She shrugged, frowned more deeply, got a sarcastic edge in her voice like the cut of a rusty shovel blade. "Oh, when she screeches like a wildcat, when she's up for anything and everything, any time of the day or night…"

This wasn't Roxanna talking, Gino realized. He could see it in her face, hear it in her voice and in the words she used. She'd been hurt, and she was mouthing the opinions of the person who'd hurt her.

"…when she can never get enough, no position too uncomfortable, no words too strong, undying slavish gratitude to her man for her gazillions of off-the-Richter-scale multiple—"

Rox stopped, closed her eyes, wished she could turn back time and paralyze the tongue that had betrayed her by turning so bitter and running on so long. Even though she couldn't see it, she knew the way Gino must be looking at her—appalled, because who wouldn't be by what she'd unleashed.

He'd spooked her badly just now when he'd talking about *something happening.* They'd kissed and they'd connected. The smell of him, the taste of him, his strength and heat and the sounds he made, all of it had felt so perfect and right, unleashing a depth of need in her that scared her. It had been scaring her for days, if she was honest. She'd known none of it had gone away after that first time—the time he'd tried to trap her.

Now she felt as if she'd just eaten the richest and most delicious serving of chocolate dessert in the world. *Fabulous, thanks, but I can't take any more. Not yet. Give my system time to recover first please, before I know if I can handle another helping.*

Oh, she was confused!

"That's not your own definition of special, Roxanna," she heard Gino say, his voice measured and slow.

"Uh, no," she had to agree, eyes still shut.

"So whose is it?"

Harlan's, of course.

"My ex-husband."

"He wanted all that from you, and he blamed you for not producing it?"

"Pretty much."

Reason Number Eighteen: "You're not that great in bed. You look like you should be, but you're not."

Which meant she failed twice in one shot. Firstly because, as outlined above, she wasn't that great in bed. Secondly because she *looked like she should be,* which would have been a matter of false advertising if she'd happened to be a sports car manufacturer.

None of this she wanted to discuss with Gino Di Bartoli, so why the heck had she let herself stray into that area?

Gino wasn't saying anything.

She opened her eyes to find out why.

"I want to offer to show you exactly why you are special," he said softly, "And exactly whose responsibility it is to score success in bed—"

"It's shared," she blurted out. "As far as I'm concerned, it should be totally shared. It should be about communication and trust and giving and no pressure."

"So you see, you *are* special, if you can say that. You already understand. I don't need to show it to you. I want to. And I will. But not yet, if you don't want to."

"Not at all, Gino. Please do not assume that I want it at all!"

"Back to that again. Why? Because you're afraid you're not special?" He lowered his voice; pitch and volume both dropped to rock-bottom caress more than sound. "How can you think that, after the way we kissed?"

Rox closed her eyes again. Was this how Francesco had come so close to seducing Rowie? If so, she didn't see how her sister had been able to resist.

She made a helpless sound, declaring her own vulnerability right out loud. Maybe she could handle another piece of chocolate heaven after all…Gino's arms slid around her, and every tiny hair on her body stood on end, while someone opened a valve in the bottom of each foot and her strength went gurgling away like water out of a bath. Her bones were made of molten fudge. Her lungs were whipped cream.

"Did you forget the way we kissed?" he asked.

"No…"

"Kiss me again, to make sure."

Rox couldn't answer, because her mouth had already opened sweetly to meet his. His tongue danced against hers, and she felt the nip and scrape of his teeth as the kiss grew deeper. His body felt so strong, the muscles of his chest like a warrior's breastplate, his shoulders and upper arms filling his black T-shirt with satisfying male bulk. He fingered the ponytail she'd scraped her hair into this morning and slid the elastic down the slippery mass of hair so that it fell and bounced around her neck and shoulders.

She wrapped her arms around him, wanting the sense of possession she got when she ran her hands over him. His back felt warm and hard, with braidings of muscle divided by the straight knots of his spine, but oh, drat, her fingers were so rough! Slipping them under the lower hem of his shirt, she felt them move like sandpaper across his skin.

"I'm sorry," she tried to say.

"Your hands?" he muttered. "I like it…" He took his mouth away, ran his own hands down her arms and captured her fingers, brought them up and kissed them, gave her a slow smile. "We'll both need a shower before lunch."

"Oh, shoot, what will Maria think?"

"We're back to that? I've told you, I don't give a damn what Maria thinks."

"I like Maria."

"I like her, too, and I respect her, and she respects me. She also respects my right to conduct my personal life the way I see fit."

"Uh."

"Yes. So can we leave Maria out of this?"

"What's *this,* Gino?"

"You know." He touched his mouth softly to her neck, making her whole body tingle. "You *know.* We want to go to bed together. Right now. And there's nothing to stop us." His breath heated her earlobe, and his musical accent made each word sound new. "Come…We'll shower, and we'll meet in your room. We'll pleasure each other…no demands, just what we want now."

"No!" She twisted away from him, heart pounding and stomach lurching sideways. "Just like that?"

"Is it just like that?" His eyes raked down her body, taking in the hard beads of her nipples visible even through her bra and top, the messy state of her hair, the stretch of skin showing at her waist where he'd slid her T-shirt higher. "Come on, Roxanna, you know how strongly this has built in us since you came here. I should have brought it into the open days ago. And you don't have to hold back to prove anything to me about your virtue. I know I'm not going to discover a woman who has given herself to every man who's ever asked, once we're together in bed."

"No! Don't you dare assume that I've already said yes to this. I don't want to be your mistress."

Why was she so shocked? It was the logical next step. It was what most people wanted once they'd kissed and generated such heat. She hadn't needed to use the word mistress. It could be a mutual, equal relationship.

Still, Rox was shocked. Because it all sounded so cool and clinical. Because it was so similar to what Francesco had proposed to her sister. Meeting in her room for sex. Knowing that Maria had enough respect and enough sense of her own role to keep Pia safely out of the way while it was happening.

Maybe Rox was naive and old-fashioned and foolishly romantic—especially for a divorcée—but she didn't want that. She *was* naive, evidently, but she wasn't naive enough to imagine that she and Gino bedding each other during their free time would lead to anything deeper.

Gino had expressed his views on marriage very clearly two weeks ago. Never, ever again. Quote, "No possibility." And marriage grew out of commitment, which grew out of faith and tenderness and respect, not out of a mutual enthusiasm for sex. And no matter how much she might long for the sex, she knew she would always need much more.

"No," she said again, backing away. "I'm not up for it, Gino. I'm sorry. I don't want to be your mistress. Find someone else."

Chapter Six

He wouldn't make the same proposition again, Roxanna decided as she walked with a rapid, emotional stride back to the *palazzo*.

She felt that she already knew Gino Di Bartoli well enough to be confident on this point. He was proud, and he was practical, and she wasn't going to kid herself. If there had been anything especially revolutionary and fantastic and earth-shattering in the way they'd kissed, it must have come from him, not from her.

He was the one with the European fire and the wide experience that came with being a highly eligible male. She was the one who only *looked* like she should be good in bed, the one who didn't live up to expectations when it came to the crunch, the one who might be crazy and naive to feel this way after such a nasty divorce, but who still believed very strongly in marriage, all the same.

Gino would find someone else if he wanted a mistress that much. He would keep Rox herself to the original terms of the agreement they'd negotiated two weeks ago. She would liaise with Rowena on the garden, and she would spend time with Pia, but the mistress deal had fallen through. Terms not acceptable to both parties.

Oh, shoot, and she really was filthy!

She slipped in through the back door which lead to the kitchen on the right and the old-fashioned scullery and laundry room on the left, wondering if Gino was close behind her or still in the far reaches of the garden. Hearing the clatter of a pot lid, she called to Maria in the rapidly improving Italian that she practiced on the gardeners every day, "I'm too dirty, Maria. I'm taking a shower before I eat."

"That's fine," Maria called back. "And Signor Gino?"

"I don't know." She hooked a finger into the back of each mud-encrusted running shoe and levered them off, left them just inside the door and headed silently upstairs in her socks before Maria could ask any more difficult questions.

Stripping in front of the bathroom mirror, she found the dusty brand marks of Gino's fingers around her waist. He must have darker finger marks on his own body from where she'd touched him. She'd been the muddy one. He'd only gotten dirty secondhand, after she'd run her hands over his face and back.

Her skin tingled at the memory of how they'd exchanged all that dirt. She could have had him in here with her right now if she'd wanted, washing it off in a shared shower before they made love. Her lower stomach clenched in a surge of need when she thought about running soap-slippery hands over him, feeling his hands on her, kissing again through a stream of hot, clean water, discovering ever more intimate levels of touch.

"Was I crazy to turn him down?" she muttered out loud.

A lot of women would have thought so, but Rox knew better. It was the right thing to have done. She didn't want to be any man's part-time lover; she wanted the real deal, the total package. Marriage to Harlan had been on his terms, and she was still picking up the broken pieces of her self-esteem. Next time, if she ever managed a next time, she had to be the one to set the boundaries and the rules, or she'd be back to square one.

Ten points for progress in self-knowledge, Rox, but self-knowledge doesn't quench the fire, does it?

The shower pressure suddenly dipped and the water went cold. She knew what had happened. At the far end of the corridor in the master bedroom, Gino was taking a shower, also, naked and slippery with streams of water running down his smooth olive skin.

Oh, damn, this was hard!

She adjusted the faucet, then dipped her head under the renewed but still tepid flow, trying to forget the way her body burned, telling herself she'd have to find a way to forget because she couldn't go on feeling like this. She was here for another eight days, and that was a long time when your heart had started beating twice as fast as usual. It was like having a disease, and diseases always ran their course somehow.

The water had run too hot now. She was done. She would let Gino have it all to himself. Toweling her body dry and dressing in fresh clothes, she hurried downstairs to have lunch in the sunroom with Pia, who could play chaperone, thank you very much, if her papa chose to eat with them today.

Gino took Pia into Siena that afternoon. He had been wanting to buy her some new clothes since Sunday, when he'd finally found time to go through everything with Maria and had discovered not a single outfit that he considered suitable for a four-year-old's playtime on a Tuscan estate. Maria had offered to take her, but he wanted to do it himself.

Would Miss Cassidy approve of what he and Pia chose together? Would Lisette?

Probably not.

Corduroy dungarees in watermelon-pink? A turtleneck with purple dinosaurs? A yellow sundress with a full skirt that Pia had begun calling her daffodil dress within two minutes of leaving the store? Red sneakers, red lady beetles, red appliquéd hearts?

It turned out that Pia liked red. And she liked jeans. They bought three pairs, with several simple little T-shirts and sweaters to wear on top. On the other hand, she wasn't remotely interested in designer labels, deferential service, exquisite workmanship or dull colors.

When they got home, she wanted to show Maria and Dr. Madison her new clothes first, and then she wanted her piano lesson.

"I think Dr. Madison is still busy in the garden, darling."

"We'll go get her." She ran off at once, calling, "Maddie? Maddie?"

Had Roxanna asked Pia to call her that? It was rather

sweet, and got around the awkward issue of who "Maddie" really was—i.e., not a doctor and not Rowena.

Gino felt a spurt of restlessness and discomfort as he strolled halfheartedly toward the door in his daughter's wake. He hoped Roxanna would be working on the far side of the wall or down in the greenhouse, and that Pia wouldn't find her.

The shopping expedition this afternoon hadn't really been as urgent as certain phone calls to the Paris office, but he'd chosen to go shopping anyhow, and he knew why. To spend time with Pia, of course, but also, more urgently, to give both himself and Roxanna some space, after this morning's muddy mess—and he wasn't talking about what had washed off him in the shower just before lunch.

He felt frustrated by Roxanna's scruples. He'd seen enough American movies and television shows to know that willing sex without long-term commitment was just as common across the Atlantic as it was in Europe. Was her objection religious, feminist or what?

He wanted to understand what made her tick in this area and how her mind worked. He'd thought that he already understood her, but he'd been wrong. Had he simply been too frank and too direct? Would she have responded better to a sneakier attempt to get her into bed? Flowers and flattery? He hadn't wanted to be sneaky, nor to slather compliments on her, the way Francesco had done with her sister.

"Come on, Maddie," he heard Pia say, and shortly afterward she appeared, dragging Roxanna by the hand, which was much cleaner this afternoon.

He met up with them in the entrance hall just outside the main salon.

"Hi," Roxanna said. "Um, Pia wants me to see her new clothes."

"Yes, I hope you weren't busy."

"My daffodil dress, and my lady beetle top," Pia said.

"Oh, they sound pretty, sweetheart! No, it's fine, Gino, the gardeners have finished for today."

"And my jeans. And my sneakers. And my T-shirts. And my dungarees."

"Good heavens! Is there anything still left in the store?"

Pia gurgled and Roxanna smiled down at her, making it possible for Gino not to have to meet her eyes. "There has been a significant depletion of stock in several stores," he said.

"A boost to the local economy. Um, and then she wants another piano lesson," Roxanna added in a quieter aside. Although she turned in his direction, she didn't meet his eye. "Is it okay that I'm giving her one every day now? Sometimes even two?"

"Yes. I'm very happy that she's so keen."

"Are we disturbing you in your office? I've been trying to schedule them late in the day."

"No, it's fine," he said, not truthfully.

The piano lesson would disturb him very much, but he would be just as disturbed by anything connected with Roxanna today, even if he could have waved a magic wand and transported her instantly back across the Atlantic. She had her hand on Pia's little head, ruffling the black curls, but then she looked up at him, preparing to utter some kind of exit line, and their eyes met.

It was so awkward. All the awareness came back, and the memories. Their kiss. The way they'd laughed about the dirt on her hands. What he'd proposed and how she'd answered him. He almost said something.

I'm sorry. It was a crude assumption on my part.

Come to dinner with me in Siena tonight. Maybe I can change your mind.

We want each other. Is there nothing in your code of behavior which allows for that to be a good thing?

She knew he wanted to speak. She was waiting for it, uncomfortable and defensive and yet every bit as aware as he was. Her breathing jerked in and out like someone counting out a jazz beat. She tucked her hair behind her ear, showing him the soft, graceful lines of her neck and wrist in an unconscious gesture of invitation. Color spread subtly on her cheeks, and he wanted to kiss that gorgeous flaming satiny skin.

But he couldn't kiss her, and he couldn't say anything. Nothing felt right.

Pia tugged at Roxanna's arm. "Come on, Maddie. Everything's upstairs on my bed. I want to get scissors and cut off the tags all by myself."

"We'll see if Maria has scissors that are safe for you."

"There are some on my desk," Gino offered. "Paper scissors. Not too sharp. She's been using them all week."

"Oh, okay. Thanks. Shall I…"

"I'll get them." He strode off, glad of the opportunity to end the uneasy moment in such a practical way. Returning, he put them into her hand and said, "The daffodil dress is my favorite."

"Yes, it sounds as if it'll make her stand out in a crowd, if we ever lose sight of her," Roxanna answered, and their eyes met again.

He realized how transparent his anxiety over Pia's

disappearance at the airport two weeks ago must have been. This woman already knew more about him than did some of the senior Di Bartoli executives whom he'd worked with for years.

"I have work to do," he muttered and turned on his heel, impatient to reach the safety of his office.

He could hear every note of the piano lesson, even with the door closed. Unfortunately, he couldn't hear Roxanna's voice as clearly. He wanted to sneak out and stand in the doorway quite openly to listen, not covertly as he'd been doing for days. He had even come up with an easy excuse—to check on Pia's talent and progress and enjoyment.

But even if that excuse had fooled Roxanna, it wouldn't have fooled Gino himself, and what was the point in giving in to an attraction that couldn't go anywhere, after the decisive way she'd turned him down?

Instead, he prowled into the kitchen, where Maria was cooking chicken with lemon and capers, and potato gnocchi in a cream-and-spinach sauce. A bit of ritual hand-slapping to the backs of his fingers went on when he made his usual attempt to sneak some tastes—he and Maria had known each other for a long time—then she fobbed him off with a bread stick, a dish of olives and some cheese. He sat at the table while he snacked and considered how best to tell her the truth about who Roxanna really was.

Delivering it straight and matter-of-factly was probably best, and the revelation was way overdue.

"Dr. Madison had a serious anxiety attack while she was in London, Maria."

The older woman raised her eyebrows and her hands.

"But she seems so much better now, since she's been back! I thought something must have happened in London, yes, with her delay there, but something good, not something like that."

"Her mother came and collected her and escorted her home to Florida. The woman we have here now isn't Dr. Madison at all. It's her twin sister, a degree-qualified teacher of music, not an expert on the history of European gardens."

Maria gave an astonished exclamation.

"Yes, you don't tend to suspect such a deception, do you," Gino agreed, "when you don't know that someone even has a twin? But I'm satisfied that their intentions are good. They simply want the project to go ahead as smoothly as before, which I am assured it will. Roxanna is leaving next Friday, and either she or her sister will be back in early summer for a final week of work. Pia doesn't need to know, nor the cleaners, nor the garden staff. But I thought that you should. This one's name is Roxanna."

"Thank you, Signor Gino. I must confess I had wondered, these past two weeks."

"If Dr. Madison had substituted her twin?" Such a suspicion seemed too prescient even for the perceptive Maria.

"No, no!" She threw up her hands again and laughed. "I wondered what had happened in London. Something very good, I thought, to have made her seem so much more alive and confident, to radiate such a different aura. 'She is in love,' I said to myself. 'But when did it happen? And with whom?' Not Francesco. He seemed to terrify her. Now it is all explained, and it makes sense. I knew something had changed, something at the heart of her. Once you get a bit of life experience like I have—

and you, Signor Gino—you can pick up a person's essence very quickly."

"Do you think so, Maria?"

"Oh, I know so. It doesn't take long to know everything that's truly important about a person if you are looking closely."

She asked several more questions. How was the real Dr. Madison, then, poor little thing? Should this one be addressed by her first name? Might both sisters return together, later in the spring?

Gino answered, but his mind had gotten caught on this idea of Maria's that you could come to know a person's essence very quickly. That might be true—it probably was—but could you know yourself and your own true desires as quickly? On the whole, he thought not. It was easier to deceive yourself than to be deceived by others.

He found this an uncomfortable observation. He almost asked Maria for her opinion on it, but then kept it to himself, the way people keep certain possessions they haven't used in a long time—stored in some little-used space because, although they probably wouldn't ever be needed, there was a slight chance that they just might.

Roxanna checked the final delivery of roses on her alphabetical list as they came off the truck on Friday morning.

Madame Alfred Carriere, Madame Hardy, Madame Isaac Pereire, Madame Legras de St. Germain. They were tough little ladies; they'd all traveled well. The *Marchioness of Londonderry* had gone missing, it seemed at first, but then Luigi discovered her hiding with *Paul Neyron* amongst someone else's load of orchard trees in the back half of the truck. Paul and the Marchionness had their almost thornless canes all tangled together.

Naughty pair.

Blatantly obvious that the two of them were having an affair.

Rox thought about making this joke to Luigi, the youngest of the three gardeners, but he didn't speak any English and she wasn't confident she could pull off the humor in her Italian. It was improving every day, thanks to frequent feverish flipping through a phrase book and dictionary, but it wasn't that good yet. Humor in another language could be touchy.

Communication of any kind in another language could be touchy, she discovered a moment later.

Luigi said a string of words to her, wearing a big grin. Since she'd just been thinking about Italian humor, she thought he was making some light, joky comment, so she nodded and grinned back and pretended she'd understood.

Oops.

Seconds later, she found herself being hauled up into the dark and now roseless back of the truck by a pair of huge gardener's hands and wrestled into an enthusiastic embrace. It turned out that she'd nodded agreement to something like, "Would you like to have sex with me in the truck? It'll only take ninety seconds, because I'm incredibly fast."

He had her work pants unbuttoned and unzipped before she could even get out, "No!", which she repeated three times for clarity.

He stopped straightaway, still grinning, and offered

to help her refasten her pants. Or at least, she hoped that was what he'd offered to do. She didn't want to consider anything else he might have meant. "No, thanks," she said.

He shrugged. "Okay." Then he came out with another string of words that she thought she understood, but wanted to make quite sure about this time.

"Say that again, Luigi?" She folded her arms in order to send the right message with her body language.

"Don't you like a little fun?" he repeated.

"Yes, but this isn't it. Don't do it again, okay?" She unfolded her arms, climbed down from the truck, brushed herself down and checked her pants. Yep, no contradictory messages being sent by the state of her zipper.

Yes, she was a little flustered, but she couldn't be too angry with a man who was still shrugging, grinning and apologetically spreading his hands, as if to say, "Okay, I respect your decision, but I had to try, didn't I?"

"Don't, Luigi. Got it?"

"Sure, sure, but you know, girls think I'm very good-looking."

"Oh, very," she drawled.

He was good-looking.

He was also nineteen.

She went around to the front cab of the truck, where a blue ribbon of cigarette smoke emerged through the open driver's side window. The driver appeared to be reading some kind of lurid detective novel to augment the entertainment value of the cigarette. She wondered whether he would have noticed the ninety seconds of rocking motion in the back of his vehicle if she had actually gone along with Luigi's idea, or if he would simply have assumed that roses were being conveyed to the ground with unusual energy and enthusiasm.

"Thanks," she told him. "Everything's unloaded and it's all correct and in good condition. Do I have to sign something? Yes?"

He held out a clipboard.

She signed it.

He left.

Luigi began to trundle the first load of roses on a big handcart up the unsealed service road that led around to the back of the *palazzo,* where the garden sheds and the greenhouse were. He wouldn't get that far, as he'd soon be turning off toward the long stretch of garden where these particular roses belonged. The handcart didn't maneuver well on the gravel, and Rox soon caught up to him.

"Fun," he said. "That's all."

"No."

"Why don't American women like fun?"

"They do."

"So—"

"But American women like to decide for themselves what's fun and what isn't. I'm sure Italian women do, too."

"It would be fun. I promise. I have never in my life disappointed a woman." His hand gesture indicated about a hundred years of wildly varied sexual experience.

"No, Luigi," she repeated, not too loudly because she was aware that beyond the approaching evergreen hedge, the other gardeners would be working…and listening.

And whether it was an Italian thing or a gardener thing or what, both the older gardeners seemed to be terrible gossips and busybodies. They'd have a field day if they knew about Luigi's proposition.

"You see, you're scared of having fun. You are scared," he announced, "of experiencing the amount of pleasure I could give you, and that it would destroy you for any other man."

"I'm not, honestly. Really. Stop talking about this."

"Let yourself live. Let yourself be."

Let yourself totally lose it, more like.

Roxanna had had enough.

"Listen, Luigi," she said. "Do you like your job? Do you want to keep it? You have asked—sort of nicely—and I have said no—very clearly—and I do not want to have sex with you. You don't need to know why. You don't need to question my decision, or try to make it a more attractive offer, or refer to everything I am missing. The answer is no. And if the question is repeated one more time, you *will* be out of a job, and that's a promise."

The Italian was a wild torrent of mistakes and hesitations, English words pronounced with an Italian accent in the hope that they meant approximately the right thing that way, wrong endings on verbs, words missed out altogether and replaced with extravagant hand gestures, sentences stopped and started again because she'd gotten totally stuck.

Rox was spluttering and red-faced by the time she'd finished. Her voice had risen to a yell, she'd forgotten all about the other gardeners, and she'd apparently managed to get Luigi rooted to the ground as firmly as the roses that he and Salvatore and Benno had been planting all morning. He was as speechless as the roses, too, and his cheeks were roughly the color of a gorgeous photo in one of Rowie's rose books, of *Henry Nevard* in full bloom.

But everyone else appeared from behind the hedge and started clapping, nodding, laughing and congratulating her as if it were a star performance.

"That's right, Meess Doctor, tell the boy!" Salvatore said.

"He has a head as big as a pumpkin, time a girl told him no for a change!" Benno agreed.

"Do you hear her, Luigi? She says no."

"This is a woman who knows what she doesn't want, and you'd better believe her."

Gino appeared last and didn't say anything, just clapped and tried not to smile. Failed miserably, by the way.

Lord, *he'd* heard her tirade, too?

Rox hadn't turned down his own recent proposition with nearly such fluency and indignation. She wished, right at this moment, that she had. He was still grinning at her. She hadn't yet seen him today, and it felt as if the sun had just come out from behind a big dark cloud. He wore dark pants and a white business shirt with rolled sleeves; he looked confident and gorgeous and did such terrible things to her balance and her strength that she would have held on to a prickly thistle for support if that had been the only thing within reach.

"Good grief, what the heck is it with you Italian men?" she yelled in an impossible mixture of Italian and English, and left the four of them to answer this unanswerable question, each in his own way, as she raced toward the house. "I need a glass of iced water *right now!*"

The gardeners stayed where they were, but Gino came after her. She knew it was him because his expensive city shoes sounded quite different from the gardeners' heavy boots on the paved garden walks. And since she did know it was him, she should probably have sped up to avoid him, but instead she slowed—not too much—and he caught up to her.

Yes, and she was glad he had, because it would be nice to talk to someone more or less rational, and in her own language.

"Your Italian is improving very quickly," he said in his almost flawless English.

"Thank you. It's obviously not, because that's how I got into the whole mess in the first place."

"What did he say to you?"

"Originally? I don't know. But I pretended I understood—I thought it was some joke about the, oh, truck driver, or something, so I nodded and smiled, and then…"

"Right. Created the wrong impression."

"Yes. Which he was slow to let go of."

"So you yelled at him."

"Basically."

"You were very impressive."

"Thanks. I think."

"So it's not just me."

"I'm sorry?"

"Whom you say no to."

They'd reached the house. The back kitchen door, to be precise. Gino stopped and leaned his hand on it, reaching almost to the high lintel at the top. Rox would have had to duck under him to get to the handle, which he didn't seem in any hurry to take hold of himself.

She gave a gusty sigh between clenched teeth. "Not you, too, Gino."

And why do you always *make the strength drain out of my legs whenever I'm near you? It's so annoying!*

"No, not me, too," he said quietly, looking down at her. *Lordy, those lashes! Those cheekbones! That mouth!* "Don't worry, I'm not planning on repeating myself the way Luigi did."

"Good."

Sort of good.

Rox's imagination suddenly presented her with an image of Gino performing a ninety-second sexual miracle next to someone else's orchard trees in the back of a truck, and she felt a huge, flooding sense of loss and disappointment about missing out on the experience, which made no sense at all.

She wanted him, yes, but she didn't want to be his mistress, whether openly or secretly. Even if neither she nor Gino actually used that word, there was a relevant, rose-related quote by Shakespeare on the subject.

"A rose by any other name would smell as sweet."

Or in this case, a softer word like *lover* could taste just as sour. She didn't want to end up hurt and discarded and put in her lowly place. In fact, she would probably have had a much easier escape from hurt if she'd gone along with Luigi because he could never have touched her in the place that really counted—her heart.

So Gino's touched my heart, already?

That's *the real problem here?*

Oh, crazy me, I'm in real trouble now!

She felt close to tears.

Gino opened the door at last. "Mmm, lunch must be ready. I can smell it."

"Where is Pia?" Rox asked, trying to distract herself. "I haven't seen her all morning."

"You've been too busy with Luigi and the truck."

She slapped his forearm with the baseball cap she'd just removed from her flattened hair. "Don't!"

He tilted his head. "Don't you think it's best to treat it like a joke, not a great drama?"

"Well, true."

"You wouldn't really want to have to sack Luigi, I hope, since the hiring and firing of staff is, in fact, my responsibility, not yours."

"Oh. Right. I didn't think of that."

"No, you didn't give yourself time. You just opened your mouth and out it all came. It was awful. I was especially shocked by your attempt to turn *have sex with* into a regular verb."

"Yes, well, I don't think the Italian program at my college was all that good, and—" She took a breath. "You're laughing at me!"

"Is that so bad?" He bent, kissed her neck and had straightened up again before she'd had time to breathe, let alone react.

"Where is Pia?" she repeated. It was more like a gasp than a question. Belatedly, her reaction to his kiss had hit, and she wanted his mouth back, there on her neck and in a dozen other places.

"She is spending the day with some of Maria's grandchildren."

"Oh, that's great!"

"Is it?"

"It's great for her to have friends. She had a ball with little Ciara the other day." He was looking at her too intently, as if she'd said something exceptional. "Kids need friends. Or they don't learn to share. Or empathize. Or—" She stopped, flustered.

I'm giving a child psychology lecture.

Why is he listening to it?

Maria appeared. "Lunch is ready, Signor Gino. I can have it on the table for you in three minutes."

"Yes, please, Maria."

"I'll wash up," Rox muttered, ducking left into the old scullery. Less than a minute later, Gino had followed her and was holding out a brimming glass. "What's this?" she demanded.

"The iced water that you wanted."

She'd forgotten. She'd gone beyond the curative power of iced water. But she thanked Gino for it anyhow and drank the entire glass without drawing breath, as a kind of punishment. "Thanks," she said again, and handed back the glass. Found his gaze fixed on her face.

"You shouldn't have been so taken by surprise with Luigi," he said, putting the glass on a shelf and leaning one hand on the heavy rim of the big sink. Rox did the same thing, at a safe distance. The thick stone felt cold.

"I should have learned about Italian men by now?"

"It's not Italian men. It's you. You're beautiful. Don't you know that? And you are so full of life. It can be misinterpreted."

"You mean, it's my fault."

"No, why put it like that? Why do you blame yourself, when no-one is accusing you? And why do you say no to something that could be so good, when you seem to me like someone who says such an energetic yes to life in general?"

"I knew it! You've decided Luigi was on to something, repeating his offer over and over, and now you're trying the same—"

"I'm not. I'm curious about you, that's all, now that I'm getting to know you better. You're more like your sister than you seemed to me at first. The same mix of creative energy and an inner doubt that neither of you needs to have."

"Rowena had a lot of health problems as a baby, Gino. Lung problems. She was in and out of the hospital. It took its toll. She wouldn't want me to give you a lot of detail."

"So we'll talk about you."

"Me? The problems came later. A bad marriage and an even worse divorce. It's funny, you can understand exactly what something like that has done to you, but understanding doesn't mean you're instantly over it."

"That's true." His voice dropped, and he repeated, "That's very true. But it's a start."

"It is. And the next step, for me, is a healthy dose of self-protection. If you want to know why the mistress thing didn't appeal, Gino…the whole discreet arrangement, Maria would understand, adults-free-to-do-what-we-want-type deal…that's the reason. I'm not ready to get hurt again. And I'm not ready to be boxed up and put on the sidelines of someone else's life. I might risk the hurt again one day, but I'd never, ever want the box. Clear?"

"Impressively so."

Silence.

They'd lived through some awkward silences before, but this one felt better. Calmer. More understanding and respect behind it. And an annoying drip coming from the faucet on the wall above the sink. Gino reached out and yanked it more tightly closed.

"Ready for lunch?" he asked.

"Are you kidding?" she joked awkwardly. "Maria's cooking? I'm ready for it at ten in the morning!"

"Shall we give her a night off tonight, though? Pia is staying with Maria's daughter until bedtime. Dress up a little and I'll take you into Siena."

"Siena?" Rox repeated stupidly.

"We can eat and, if we leave here early, I can show you something of the town, since you should play the tourist a little while you are here, and we are running out of time. A courtesy, Roxanna, not anything dangerous. *Not* a repeat of my earlier offer. Especially after what you've just said."

"Should I believe you?"

"I've already told you, I'm not Luigi. I'm almost twice his age, for a start, and with much more self-control. So, dinner in Siena?"

She still couldn't answer, just narrowed her eyes and looked at him, totally at sea and horrified at how much she wanted to say yes.

Chapter Seven

They left the house at five, when the *palazzo,* the Chianti vineyards and the hills were still bathed in late sunshine, as were the rust-colored bricks of Siena's perfectly preserved and centuries-old buildings when they reached the town. Vehicle access was very restricted, but Gino had a parking arrangement at a friend's garage just outside the old city.

He'd warned Rox to wear comfortable shoes, which limited her choice to a pair of flat black leather sandals that Rowena had left behind. She had to fold up an extra hem on Rowie's black trousers, pin it with safety pins and press it in place in order not to scuff the fabric on the ground, and she had to match it with the same pink jacket of her sister's that she'd worn two weeks ago.

Yes.

The kiss jacket.

Except I'm not going to call it that.

Once these wardrobe crises had been dealt with, however, she stopped caring that she wouldn't be the best-dressed woman in Italy tonight and fell in love with Siena instead.

"Where are the strip malls and the gas stations and the billboard advertising?" she asked Gino. "Are you telling me no-one's built anything new in this town since the fourteenth century?"

He laughed. "They have, but they've obviously done a good job of making it blend in, if that's your reaction. There's a very strict code about what's allowed."

"It's so beautiful. It looks as if it just grew out of the ground."

"I suppose in a way it did, and I'll take some personal credit for it, too, since one branch of my family helped to govern this town six hundred years ago."

"Personal credit for things your ancestors did? I hope they weren't big into pillage and torture, then."

"Not too much of that, from what we can work out."

"The brick is so warm to look at. There's a paint color called burnt sienna…"

"Yes, that's the one. Because of the color of the local clay."

"I'm not going to talk anymore, I'm just going to look. Do you mind? Is there an itinerary before we eat, or can we just walk?"

He laughed again. "We can just walk. There's no itinerary, and I'm not itching to give a running commentary."

Rox looked and listened and smelled. People had begun to cook for the evening, and the weather was mild enough that windows and doors were open here and there, treating her to aromas that reminded her of Maria's wonderful meals. An old man in a faded black coat rode past them on a bicycle. Pigeons cooed and squabbled in an alleyway. Someone standing high above her in an attic room practiced the violin, the cascading notes of a familiar passage seeming to call to her well after she and Gino had passed on.

After about twenty minutes, she told him, "Okay, now you can talk if you want. Tell me more about your ancestors, and what happens here now. There must be festivals and markets, a million tourists."

"Well, there are the horse races in the summer…" he began.

They didn't stop to eat until eight, by which time Rox was hungry enough to want everything on the restaurant menu, yet happily sated with history and architecture and art. "I can't choose," she told Gino helplessly. "It all sounds so good, and the walk was so good. I just can't."

"That's out of character, Roxanna," he teased her gently. "You usually give the impression that you know exactly what you want. Or what you don't want, in the case of Luigi."

"We're never going to hear the end of that episode, are we, either of us? It'll haunt Luigi until Salvatore and Benno retire, and I'll only escape by crossing an ocean. Okay, I'm going to go with acting out of character, Gino. You choose for me."

"You think I want such responsibility?"

"I think you were born to it."

He shrugged. "Then it's my destiny."

They ate appetizers of fresh marinated anchovies and

a plate of *crostini*—rounds of toasted Italian bread spread with olive paste or marinated red pepper or marsala-flavored pâté. For their entrées, Gino chose quail wrapped in vine leaves and a rich venison casserole. He was impressed when Rox announced that she still had space for dessert.

"I'm not going to suggest *panforte,* even though it's Siena's best-known specialty, because Maria makes a better one than I've ever had elsewhere," he said, "but there's a good Florentine dessert they do at this restaurant, called *zuccotto,* full of chocolate and almonds and hazelnuts and cream, which—"

Chocolate, nuts and cream? Stop right there!

"Yes. I'll have that."

It was nearly eleven before they were ready to leave. Rox hadn't had very much wine, but Gino had ordered one of Tuscany's best reds and she found a small glass went a long way. Or maybe it wasn't the wine at all; maybe it was just fatigue after today's work in the garden and the long walk around Siena's streets, and the total sensory overload of this place.

Walking back along the dark and now chilly streets, then beyond the oldest part of the city toward the converted stable where they'd garaged Gino's car, all she could think about was the fact that he would probably try to kiss her at some point between here and her bedoom door.

Of course he would.

She'd fall on the ground in a screaming heap if he didn't.

And she couldn't let him do it, so she'd better start working on her escape strategy right now.

Not logical, Rox.

Harlan had pointed out to her that she wasn't logi-cal—Reason Number Twenty—but logic wasn't the same thing as common sense, and tonight it made total sense that she could want Gino to kiss her with every cell in her body even though she knew she had to stop him if he tried.

Maybe I should kind of maneuver into the right position for it, she thought, *so that he'll make his move and I can get the saying no part over with sooner.*

All right, bad line of reasoning there.

Don't move closer to him, Rox. That really would be illogical.

His shoulder cruised along beside her, roughly level with her ear. She could so easily have pillowed her head there, or just tipped it over a little and bumped him, so he would have put an arm around her to steady her. Then surely he would have kept it there, all warm and heavy and strong.

But she didn't do it. She stayed where she was, and so did he. He smiled at her when they reached the car, but that was all.

It was enough. Her whole body had gone soft and tingly with wanting him. Without even looking at him, she knew exactly where he was and the way he held his body. Her legs felt shaky as she slid her backside across the buttery leather of the Ferrari's seat, and her pulses throbbed. She hadn't known that desire could feel so physical, so dizzying, so wonderful, or that a smile could melt a woman like ice cream in a frying pan.

When Gino had walked around the long front of the car and opened his own door, she watched him slide

closer to her and felt her stomach drop with disappointment when they didn't touch. He smiled at her again as
he started the engine and that made her stomach jump
back up again so far, crazy thing, that it collided with
her galloping heart. She smiled back at him, light-
headed with happiness.

"Did you have a good time?" he asked as they drove.

"You know I did."

"I like to hear you say it."

"How many times? I'll make a note."

"I like the different ways you've said it. I like the way
you enjoy yourself, Roxanna. It's…what's the word in
English? Infectious?"

"That's right."

Okay, so he's still working up to it, she thought.
*That nice compliment just now, about liking the way I
enjoy myself. And the smiles. I can see it coming, but
he's going to wait. Maybe in the dark, just beside the
garage, with enough light spilling from the house so I
can see his face and those gorgeous dark eyes. Maybe
not until we're inside. In the kitchen…He'll offer me a
glass of water. Or in the front hall, if we go that way.
Or maybe upstairs.*

But they got all the way from the garage, through the
front door, up the stairs and along the corridor as far as her
room, and the only kiss was the one Rox kept rehearsing
in her head, the one she wasn't going to let him give her.

He stopped at her door. "I'm going to change and do
a little work downstairs," he said. "Thank you again for
your company this evening. I enjoyed every minute."

He cupped his hand and touched the side of her face,
the movement so light that it felt like the brush of tissue

paper. She caught a featherlight drift of his scent, that mix of wine and leather and soap and coffee that always seemed so familiar and perfect.

"I'll see you in the morning." His voice was very low, then he turned and soon disappeared.

Ug.

That was *it?*

That was the Attack of the Expert Kisser she'd been planning how to fend off for the past hour?

Rox sagged against the bedroom door, then opened it just enough to slither weakly inside. Her whole body crawled with disappointment, and metal bands began to tighten around her head as the questions came.

Did Gino know what she had expected and wanted and planned to fight off? Had he guessed that she hadn't trusted his promise not to act like Luigi and repeat his offer over and over in the expectation of getting a different answer?

"Get real, Roxanna Madison," she muttered. "You weren't going to say no, were you? Not for a second. If he'd kissed you, you would have kissed him back like crazy."

She'd been virtually loosening up her lips in preparation the whole way home. In the back of her mind—being totally honest here—her only genuine piece of strategic thinking had been the question of how long she could kiss him for and then still say no to the mistress thing the next time he asked.

Illogical.

Harlan, I owe you an apology. I need to glue that list of yours to the mirror. You're probably right about every item on it.

With grim efficiency, she prepared for bed, and then lay awake for four hours, seriously wondering if she should slip along the corridor to Gino's room, let herself in and wake him with the news that she'd changed her mind.

She didn't do it.

In the morning, Rox discovered via Maria that Gino's sister-in-law had arrived the previous evening from Rome for a weekend visit while she and Gino had been playing tourist in Siena. Lisette Falconi had parked her brand-new BMW in a locked shed behind the main garage, so they hadn't seen it on their return.

She'd brought her daughter Nicoletta, whom Rox met over breakfast and could only coax a few words from, never mind a smile. Lisette apparently was still in bed. The child seemed sullen and awkward, despite her inheritance of classic Parisienne good looks, and she already possessed a teenager's hormonal hostility even though she'd only just turned twelve.

They were staying until early Tuesday morning. Their arrival shouldn't have thrown Rox off-kilter, but somehow it did, because she instinctively knew that she wouldn't get another shot at the mistress deal now.

As, except in her very weakest moments, she had had no intention of ever saying yes to the mistress deal, her lead-stomached disappointment set a new benchmark for illogical behavior, which she could only attempt to deal with by spending as much of the day as possible hiding with Pia in the garden.

"I told you on Thursday that I might come, and I phoned here yesterday afternoon to say I definitely would," Lisette told Gino over breakfast. She gave an apologetic smile. "Maria said you'd just left."

Since she had a standing invitation to visit whenever she wanted to, and since he knew he hadn't been listening to her properly over the phone on Thursday, Gino couldn't very well object.

And he wasn't quite sure why he wanted to. He'd been grateful for Lisette's input in the past. After the divorce, Angele had teasingly suggested that he might have been better off with her sister instead. He always assumed she hadn't been serious. Lisette had already been married when he and Angele had met.

In fact, that was *how* they had met. He'd known Lisette first. Angele had been in Rome visiting her sister, and Lisette's husband had business connections with the Di Bartoli Corporation.

"It's good to see you, Lisette," he told her, inwardly poking at his emotions like poking a heap of ash in search of any remaining heat. "Do you have any definite plans? Does Nicoletta?"

"I want to see the garden, of course. Will you give me a tour after breakfast? You and that shy little American? I don't suppose the gardeners are working today."

"No, they're not, and the garden is looking very unfinished, a lot of imagination is still required, but of course I'll show it to you."

"How is the little American? Living up to her qualifications?"

"She's not little, for a start."

"Oh, you know what I mean, Gino. I only met her once, here with Francesco, but I must have terrified her somehow, because the only time she didn't shrink back like a mouse was when she was talking about the garden. Then, yes, I could understand what Francesco saw in her. She had a lovely creative energy and she was obviously quite bright, but I couldn't help feeling sorry for her."

"Well, that's history, now."

"With Francesco?"

"There's been a change of plan." He briefly summarized Dr. Madison's breakdown, and her twin's new role in seeing the project through, and although Lisette raised her eyebrows, he glossed over Roxanna's initial deception and presented the story the way he'd have presented growth projections at a board meeting—with utter confidence in how it would all play out.

Lisette was satisfied enough to change the subject. "And how is my darling Pia? Missing Miss Cassidy, I expect."

The casual comment brought Gino up short and focused his thinking like a crystal focusing the sun's rays. Pia hadn't mentioned Miss Cassidy since she had been here.

Not once.

Not to him, anyhow.

He must ask Maria and Roxanna…

He must give Miss Cassidy her notice as soon as he could get hold of her, because his little girl *should* be missing the person who cared for her every day. If Pia didn't miss her, then Miss Cassidy was the wrong person for the job.

"Gino?" Lisette said.

"Sorry. Thinking."

"Nicoletta will play with her like a big sister. At least— Has she been having many of her tantrums?"

"No, not for days. She's settled down here so well—
Roxanna has been giving her music lessons—I'm seriously wondering about not taking her back to Rome."

But how can I manage that?

He dropped into thought again, aware of the patient,
sisterly way Lisette was watching him but just not able
to provide the kind of small talk she wanted right now.

Chapter Eight

"Where is that little girl? Where is Pia? Is she under this bench? No…Is she behind this tree? No…"

Rox and Pia were playing hide-and-seek, and the game would have been over five minutes ago if Rox had pounced on Pia when she first spotted her after opening her eyes. The little red-sleeve-covered elbow sticking out from behind the base of the marble fountain tended to draw a person's attention.

But by this time, Rox knew from experience that Pia didn't like to be found too soon. What four-year-old did? And she loved it when Rox made an exaggerated performance out of her quest, looking in the silliest and most impossible places.

"I really do think she might be under this pot," Rox said, upturning a cylinder of terra-cotta that could barely have fit a newborn kitten. "No…"

Pia giggled.

"Now, where did that sound come from? Was it a bird? No, I'm sure it was Pia laughing, but where is she?"

One of the gardeners had left a pickax under the hedge. Rox hefted it by a wooden handle worn to satin by years of use, and decided to "discover" Pia on her way to the toolshed to put the pickax away.

During the course of the hide-and-seek game she'd managed a useful amount of checking over the previous week's work, and she thought Rowie would be pleased. They were well up to schedule, and in Florida Rowena had written half the text for the plaques. She was still researching their actual design, wanting something practical and long-wearing that would be in keeping with the garden's overall mood. From the sound of her voice on the phone, she was obviously enjoying the whole process.

And she'd found a therapist whom she really liked.

There was a song that fitted Rox's mood, out here in the fresh morning air, but she could only remember a snatch of it. *Everything's coming up roses...*

"Pia! I've found you! At last!"

"You were so funny, Maddie. Don't you see how little that flowerpot is?"

"Well, I was pretending a bit, there, sweetheart. It's fun making people laugh."

Voices sounded and feet crunched on the gravel. Gino had brought Lisette and Nicoletta outside to show them the garden. Nicoletta still seemed sullen and bored, and didn't respond to Pia's cute entreaties to continue the game of hide-and-seek.

Lisette seemed unaware. "Oh, this gorgeous sun!"

she said. "I'm going to do nothing but lie in it asleep all day like a cat."

Gino made introductions. His focus slipped past Rox's face too quickly, and his hand hovered near her shoulder for a moment as if he didn't know what to do with it. She knew her breathing wasn't quite steady, and that she was going to have the same problem as Gino about finding the right places to look, and the right way to hold her body.

Imagine if she'd gone to his room last night to offer him what he wanted, and Lisette had glimpsed her empty bed, or seen her emerge from Gino's room this morning. Imagine if Pia had! There were a dozen innocent, giveaway lines a four-year-old could have come out with on that subject.

Lisette shook Rox's hand—fortunately the one that was still clean, because she'd been holding the gardener's grubby pickax in the other—and murmured, "I hear we're to call you something different now."

Rox smiled, still so aware of Gino standing there, listening to this. "Pia calls me Maddie," she said.

Lisette raised her delicate eyebrows. "Gino, what do you call her?" she asked.

"Roxanna. But I like Maddie, too."

Lisette's eyes narrowed for a moment. "Oh, do you? You don't find it too familiar, on Pia's part? I hate inviting disrespect in a child." She glanced between Gino and Rox, and apparently saw something she didn't like. Her smile grew wider and so did her eyes, but her white teeth fitted together just a little too tightly. "Poor Pia…" she murmured.

Lisette left the other adults to assume why Pia should

be pitied; fortunately, the little girl herself wasn't listening. She was still trying to find a game that Nicoletta might like.

"Can you climb trees?"

"No. I'm not a kid. I don't play kiddy games."

Strike three, and Nicoletta was out. Pia's forehead knitted up in a thunderous frown that no-one had seen for days. She started throwing little bits of gravel.

"Not on the pretty green grass, darling," Lisette told her, but then didn't seem to notice when Pia kept on throwing. Most of her attention was focused on Gino.

Nicoletta turned to her mother to ask in an indignant stage whisper if she had to play with a baby all weekend because if so, she was going to be bored out of her mind and she'd never come here again. Lisette promised a gift if Nicoletta was good.

"I must put this in the shed," Rox said.

"We'll come with you," Gino told her. He turned to Pia. "Come with us, darling." He watched as she forgot about throwing the gravel, thank goodness. Then he spoke to Rox again. "Lisette wants a tour. Would you like to tell her the change in our thinking, since it was your idea."

"Right. Um, you see…" Rox outlined the changed garden design concept, but it was hard to share the magic since Lisette looked almost as bored as her daughter.

"Wonderful," she murmured a couple of times, but she could have been talking about the sun on her back.

She was perfectly groomed, but her heeled, strappy shoes didn't work on the gravel or the grass. She was beautiful, too, laying a proper claim to that word in a way that Rox never could. Gorgeous bone structure, wide-spaced dark eyes, perfect brows and lips and neck, hair that was either a natural glossy mink-brown or dyed by a world-class professional. Gino had mentioned that Angele and Lisette's mother had been American, but Lisette seemed so European that Rox would never have guessed.

"Gino, you're going to have a hard time keeping me away from here this summer," Lisette said. "I'll be with you every weekend. I've been telling you for years how spectacular this garden could be if it was treated as a showpiece for the corporation. Will you admit now that I was right?" She laid her hand on his bare forearm and gave him a little caress.

A big, thick serpent of jealousy uncoiled itself inside Rox's stomach. She wanted to step forward like an angry schoolteacher and say, *Excuse me? Aren't you married, Mrs. Falconi? Keep your hands to yourself!*

"I admit you were right," Gino answered his sister-in-law in a lazy voice. "I admit we should have done this years ago."

"Good." Lisette moved into sexy pout mode with her smile.

The snake in Rox's stomach stretched and started slithering around. Gino must like this flirty treatment. If he was just being polite, or oblivious, no-one would have guessed. Pia ambled toward the house, throwing her bits of gravel again. They pinged off the side of the fountain and chinked on a huge terra-cotta urn that would be planted with summer annuals in a few weeks. Maria would soon get her cheerful again inside the house.

The garden tour continued along the outside of the old wall that ran parallel to the adjacent Chianti vines, their rows lusciously green and perfectly straight. Nicoletta gave an update on her boredom level.

Climbing, everyone. Just thought you'd all want to know. I'm twelve, I can get dangerous.

"Put on a DVD," Lisette said vaguely, then to Gino, with her hand back on his arm, "Shall we ask Maria to bring us something cool to drink? Roxanna, could you do that for us?"

Coupled with a polite, shuttered smile, this final question put Rox in her place and indicated that only two glasses would be required. She said, "Yes, of course."

"On the terrace, thank you," Lisette said.

"Coming right up…" But as Rox spoke, she saw Gino give a little frown and understood that he wasn't happy about the role Lisette had assigned to her. He considered Rox to be somewhat more significant in his life than a drink waitress.

So there, Lisette!

The snake in Rox's stomach lay back and basked in the sun, as she set off back along the wall and around to the house. She hated the snake!

Is this a contest? I've already turned down the prize. Why am I thinking this way?

Lisette was welcome to Gino. The mistress arrangement he'd offered Roxanna would suit the other woman perfectly—a discreet liaison that need provide no threat to her marriage at all, since neither she nor Gino would ever want to publicly change the status of their relationship.

"Maria," she said in the kitchen, "Lisette and Gino would like something cool to drink outside. Do you know what she usually has? Oh, and I guess Nicoletta, also."

"Not you, Meess Maddie?"

I wasn't asked.

"I'm going to check what Pia's doing," Rox said out loud. "Do you know where she is?"

Maria opened her hands and made one of her clucking sounds. "She's not outside, with you?"

"No, she came in a while ago. I thought she'd come straight to you."

"No, she didn't. I wonder… Let me take out the drinks, and you can call her. She's very quiet."

So quiet that Rox couldn't find her. "Pia?" she called. "Where are you?"

No answer.

She inspected several of Pia's favorite indoor hiding places, which she knew well by this time. No luck. She glanced into Gino's office, toured the dining room, looked behind various doors upstairs, calling at intervals.

This was hide-and-seek for real, but maybe Pia didn't know that. "I'm not playing any more, darling," she called. "You have to tell me where you are."

Still no answer.

Maria had come back from serving the drinks. "Could she have gone out again without me hearing? After all, I didn't hear her come in."

"But I didn't see her outside on my way from the rose wall. Does Gino know we're looking for her? I know he doesn't like there to be any risk of her getting lost."

"I'll tell him. It's not like her to wander as far as the main road, but— He would never forgive us." She shook her head. "Never forgive himself."

Maria went back outside and Rox climbed the stairs again, to start a more thorough search of the house. Pia probably thought this was still a game. Could she have fallen asleep in a closet or under a bed?

She heard voices and footsteps. Lisette, Maria and Nicoletta had come back into the house, while Gino was searching outside. She heard his voice calling, "Pia? Pia? Darling, you must answer us!"

And then she heard an angry shriek downstairs and a sharp tirade of words from Lisette. It was still going on when Rox reached Gino's office. "You destructive, wasteful, psychopathic child! Give me that, this second! You are a terrible, wicked little girl!"

Rox froze in the doorway, horrified. Lisette pulled one way on Pia's daffodil dress while Pia herself pulled on the other, and Lisette was stronger so Pia slowly got dragged out from under Gino's desk, refusing to let go.

She still had scissors in her hand, and from the sight of the dress's ragged hem, she'd apparently been cutting it into a fringe. Considering she was using paper scissors, she'd made amazing progress. She was red-faced, tearful and screaming so that Rox's ears rang, but it was the adult's anger that seemed most frightening, not the child's.

Lisette's furious tirade continued. "What are you doing, you destructive, terrible girl? You have ruined your dress." She turned to Roxanna, still yelling. "You can see it, can't you? She is very disturbed. She must be. Seriously disturbed. To try to punish poor Gino this way! She's monstrous!"

Was Pia listening to this? That was Rox's first thought.

No, thank goodness. She was crying way too loudly to hear anything coming from anyone else.

"I'm not sure that it's punishment, Lisette," Rox said.

And I'm quite sure that yelling at her and blaming her and calling her disturbed *and* monstrous *right in front of her is not the way to go here. What would Gino think about what you're saying? I wish he were here, because I can't confront you on it.*

But I can do something for Pia, she realized. *That's what's really important.*

"Pia, sweetheart—" she began, then stopped, knowing Pia wouldn't hear. She needed to take this slower and more gently.

The screaming continued, and Rox lowered herself to the floor and silently began stroking the palm of her hand down Pia's back. With her attention fully focused on the little girl, she didn't even see Gino come in.

"What on earth is going on?" he said, his whole body like a magnet in the doorway. He nudged Lisette aside and she let him into the room, her eyes fixed on him, wide and innocent and scared.

"Oh, Gino!" she moaned. She pressed her hands to her face, as if to squeeze her betraying anger away, and her voice dropped to an anguished whisper. "Look at how she has ruined her dress, the poor darling." She picked up the dress, shook it, threw it down, then caressed Pia's hair with a gentleness she hadn't shown a few minutes ago. She ignored the scissors still in the child's grasp. "I don't know what is going on in this sweet little head."

Rox didn't buy Lisette's change of attitude for a second, but she did sense a tiny slackening of tension in Pia's body, and that was what counted. "Give me the scissors, darling," Rox said quietly, coaxing them out of the small, clenched fist.

"What happened to make her do this?" Gino muttered, helpless as he'd been at Rome airport two and a half weeks ago. Even more anguished—or could Rox just read him better now?

"You must see that Meess Cassidi is right about these tantrums, Gino," Lisette said. "Pia needs a very clear, strong strategy, and we must persevere. Nicoletta was never like this. Look at what she has done, poor sweetheart. We must follow through consistently until—"

"No," Gino answered on a sigh. "No, Lisette, I'm not doing it that way any more."

"You can't possibly *reward* this behavior! We can't have our darling Pia—"

He sighed between his teeth. "No, but I must at least try to understand it, and how can I do that if I simply—"

"You're giving in to her! Oh, no, Gino, darling, I don't believe it, after all Meess Cassidi's months of work. Is this fair to Pia?"

Gino put his arm absently around Lisette's shoulders, turned a little. "Roxanna?"

She felt just as helpless as he did. Pia was still screaming. From Lisette's cooing tones and anxious expression, you never would have known how she'd yelled a few minutes earlier. Gino definitely didn't know. Had he ever seen that streak in the personality of Pia's aunt?

Let me tell you what she said, Gino, what words she used about your daughter. How can I, though? You'd have to have heard it for yourself…

"Calm her first?" Rox suggested, looking up at him and mouthing the words. "Find out *why,* because she loves this dress, and I would have thought—"

"Yes. She does love it," he agreed. "Lisette, I think

three adults in the room are too many. Come, we'll see if Roxanna can calm her down."

"Well, I certainly don't want my ears ringing for the rest of the day. Poor sweetheart." She added the last two words a little too quickly.

Gino still had his hand on her shoulder as they left the office.

Rox let Pia go on screaming for a minute or two. She didn't say anything, she just sat there and made sure that the child wasn't going to hurt herself throwing her little body about. When Pia paused to draw in a shuddery breath, Rox asked casually, "Are you getting hungry, Pia? Maria's going to make you a boiled egg for lunch." She knew Pia loved dipping fingers of bread into the rich yellow yolk.

Pia didn't answer, but the force of her screaming had eased.

"Your dress is just about the same color as egg yolk, isn't it?"

The cries were more shudder than scream, now.

"I love this color," Rox said. "It's like flowers, and the sun, and cheese."

"And tortellini," Pia added.

"And tortellini," Rox agreed, "Maria's special kind." She waited a moment, then asked carefully, "Why did you cut your beautiful dress, darling?"

"I'm getting good at cutting. I've been doing cutting with Papa before breakfast."

"Yes, you're very good at cutting. So was that why? Were you practicing? You should have practiced on a piece of paper, sweetheart."

"I wanted it to look better like a daffodil. I looked at

them in the big tub by the gate. They have frilly edges, and I wanted frilly edges on my daffodil dress."

"So you weren't doing it because you were angry?"

Dumb question, Rox.

Pia can't analyze her own feelings that way.

She's four.

Rox tried again. "Did you have a nice morning? We played hide-and-seek, but then I had to show everyone the garden, didn't I? And I think you were still playing hide-and-seek in the house when I was calling you."

"I was bored outside. Nicoletta wouldn't play. But Aunt Lisette didn't like the frilly edges. *She* was the one who was angry. Very angry."

"Did you get scared, darling?"

"Yes, and angry back at her. She wouldn't let me finish. She grabbed the dress and pulled. Daddy says I shouldn't grab. I wanted to do the cutting all the way round, to look nice, but she wouldn't let me. Do you like the frilly edges, Maddie?"

Oh lordy, do I tell her she's ruined the dress? She thinks she's done something wonderful. She doesn't understand about raw edges fraying in the wash.

"They're lovely, darling," Rox answered, her mind working away like a rattly machine. "So straight! You really are good at cutting now."

I could let her finish all the way around, she thought, *make sure none of her cuts go up too far. The dress comes well below her knees, and her frilly bits are only a few inches. I could cut it all off, turn up a new hem, sew the fringe bit back on, an inch or two above the hem. The fringe would still fray, but it wouldn't fray the whole dress. It's a play-dress, after all. She's not wearing it to a ball.*

"Let's finish it, Pia, and I'll hold it while you cut, to help you."

They emerged from Gino's office after twenty minutes of painstaking work, during which Rox had also explained to Pia that she must never, never do cutting without asking a big person first, and that when the seeker said it wasn't a game anymore, then the hider had to call or come out. The salt marks from Pia's dried tears were still visible on her face.

Gino and Lisette had been waiting outside, finishing their drinks on the terrace, seated in white wrought iron chairs, and Rox felt a spurt of dislike for the other woman. *Don't trust her, Gino. She yells at Pia when you're not around. She pretends she cares about your daughter, but I don't think she does. Not in a way that's good for Pia, anyhow.*

Or was this just the voice of the jealous snake still slumbering deep inside her?

"Well, we're quiet, at least," Lisette murmured, when she saw Rox and Pia.

Gino stood up and came toward them. "Any answers?" he mouthed to Rox.

"One very simple answer, involving the desire to more closely resemble a daffodil," she told him quietly, leaving out her opinion that the tantrum element was as much Lisette's problem as Pia's. "As far as Pia was concerned, Gino, it was a creative act, not a destructive one."

"But the new dress is ruined."

Rox explained what she planned to do with it—it would work; Maria had a sewing machine—and Gino lifted his head and laughed. "Between the two of you, that's as much creativity as I can handle for one

morning. We have our hands full around here, Maria and
I. Are you listening to this, Lisette?"

"Yes, I am," she answered at once, pasting on a
bright smile. "And I'm taking you out to lunch on the
strength of it. We are both in sore need of a break, you
and I." Her voice dropped to a huskier note. "Especially
you, so if you're planning to argue the idea, Gino,
don't!"

Are you planning to argue, Gino? Rox wondered.
Can't you see what she wants? Please argue...

That nasty, jealous snake slithered around in her
stomach again, and for the first time she found herself
thinking, *I'm scheduled to leave in less than a week. Six
days. Only that long, thank heaven. I can stop falling in
love with Gino then, because I'll never see him again.*

Gino Di Bartoli.

The man who wanted a mistress but never a wife.

The man who already had Rox's heart, but who
would probably choose two-faced, yelling Lisette
instead, because he didn't want a woman's whole, extravagant, messy heart, but only her body.

"Lunch," Gino said. "Yes, that would be perfect." He
added formally, "Thank you very much, Lisette."

He arranged things with Maria, and Lisette disappeared upstairs to change. The two of them roared off
in his red Ferrari half an hour later, with relieved smiles
on their faces and barely a backward glance, Nicoletta
sulked in the sunroom with a sandwich and a DVD,
while Rox and Pia ate bread fingers dipped in golden
egg yolk in the kitchen.

Maria had already gone to a little room tucked
behind the main staircase to set up the sewing machine,

and the snake in Rox's stomach had deflated like a pricked balloon because there was no point in feeling jealous of the winner when you discovered you'd never even been seriously in the race.

Chapter Nine

There was a music lesson in progress when Gino and Lisette returned home at four from their long, lazy restaurant lunch. Gino himself had suggested the idea to Maria a couple of days earlier. "If any of your grandchildren come over on the weekend, see if you can get Roxanna to do a little music with them."

He hadn't let Maria in on his thinking: Roxanna still didn't believe she'd make a good teacher; after listening to her teach his daughter for two weeks, Gino was even more convinced that she would.

And his ego got a little itchy if he wasn't given the chance to prove himself right. He liked being right. He privately admitted to this personal flaw and went right ahead and gave in to it every time.

Taking a quick peek into the airy room, he saw Roxanna pound out a cheerful rhythm on the piano, then pause while four pairs of feet echoed the same rhythm back to her. "That's great!" she said, dropping her fingers into a lighter background beat. "Keep going."

She played a different rhythm, and the children copied it again. Every cheek was flushed and every eye was bright, Roxanna's included. Even Nicoletta was here, not exactly joining in—she was slumped sideways in an armchair, with her bent knees hooked over one side—but listening and secretly tapping with her fingers to prove that she could copy the rhythm correctly, a lot better than a bunch of silly little kids.

"Fabulous, guys! I'm going to do some trickier ones, now. See if you can stomp your feet when I go down low—" Roxanna attacked the deepest octaves on the instrument "—and clap your hands when I come up high." *Tinkle-clunk, tinkle-clunk* went the top keys.

Over lunch, Gino had realized how much he was destined to disappoint her. That hum, that curl, that entire *symphony* of awareness still existed between them, stronger every day, but he wouldn't ever be able to satisfy her in bed because she was the all-or-nothing type—he admired that about her, if he were honest with himself—and she wouldn't go to bed with him unless he offered her a whole lot more.

He couldn't offer her more. How could he? But at least he could give her something—a belief in herself as a teacher, and the glimpse of new possibilities for a future career if she had to turn her back on singing. She was only here for another week...slightly less, in fact...and it was strange, very strange, that he really wanted to say goodbye to her knowing he'd enriched her life, made her heart and her spirit stronger and happier.

She deserved that. She was an incredible person, and he wanted her to realize it.

He didn't feel the same way about Lisette; he didn't have the same need to give.

Which was good.

His sister-in-law had given him a little shock over lunch, and he was still thinking back on it, wondering why he hadn't seen it coming. In hindsight, she'd given a few signals.

"It's impossible out here in the country, isn't it?" she'd said lazily as they ate, fingering the stem of her wineglass. "Far too many peasants."

"Peasants?"

"You act like a peasant yourself, Gino, when you're here. Encouraging Maria to have her children and grandchildren drop in, chatting with Benno and Salvatore. In Rome, it would be different. We could arrange things. You know what I mean."

And suddenly he *had* known.

He'd nodded slowly, taking refuge in his wine, and she'd continued with a new light in her eyes, "We could be very discreet. No interruptions. Oh, I know Maria would see to it that we had no interruptions here if you asked her to, but it wouldn't be the same."

"No?" He'd still been at a loss at this point, too surprised to act decisively. He'd always thought that her open fondness for him—yes, even with those little caresses—was an extension of her closeness to Angele, or at the very most a bit of light, meaningless flirtation.

"No, it wouldn't be the same at all," she'd repeated with a pout. "I had been thinking that this weekend we might… But no, we'll wait till you're back in Rome, shall we?"

She'd smiled at him, her lids half lowered, and he couldn't help smiling back. He'd depended on her so much since Angele's death. He would never want to hurt or offend her, even when her proposition was out of the question.

Was it so out of the question? He ought to examine the idea, at least for a few minutes, he'd decided in a thickheaded way. She was offering exactly what he wanted, wasn't she? The same thing he'd offered to Roxanna—the simple pleasure of a no-strings-attached affair, with the spice of secrecy sprinkled on top.

And he knew her—her family, her background, her way of thinking. Her parents had conducted affairs of this type for years. Currently based in Singapore, they were still together but led very separate lives, and so far had shown little interest in either of their granddaughters, even after Angele's death. Lisette was similarly cool and practical. There would be no unpleasant surprises down the road. She wouldn't suddenly want to change the rules.

But she's married, he'd thought. *I'm not an adulterer.*

And haven't you begun to notice, since you've known Roxanna, that Lisette doesn't actually understand Pia very well, a new little voice inside him had added.

Lisette would have argued that the whole concept of adultery as a sin was an idea for peasants and that the issue of Pia was quite irrelevant. Since when did a mistress need to understand her lover's child?

He hadn't given her a clear answer to her question over lunch. He just hadn't been able to find the right way to say no. But Lisette must have been satisfied with his uncertain smile because she hadn't pushed, she'd just picked up her wineglass and asked him to pour her some more.

"Okay, that's enough, everyone," Roxanna said, at the piano. "My fingers need a break."

"No! More!" said four little voices in Italian. "We want more!"

"Nope, not today," she told them cheerfully. Then she stood up, turned and saw Gino.

Did her flushed cheeks get pinker? He thought so, and he was pleased, which was wrong of him, he realized. He should take the initiative in keeping his distance; he shouldn't look for evidence that their connection was still there. Was it really Pia he'd been thinking about over lunch? Or Roxanna and the changes she had brought out in his daughter?

"You're not going to give them any more?" he asked her as she came toward him.

"Treat 'em mean, keep 'em keen, that's my educational philosophy," she said. The gaggle of younger children tumbled past her and out of the room.

"I'm hungry," Gino heard.

Nicoletta drifted in their wake and managed a smile at Roxanna on her way past.

"If I go on until I get boredom vibes from them," Roxanna said, "they might remember the boredom next time, not the fun they had at first. We've been in here for forty-five minutes. That's enough."

"I don't know why you think you're not good at this."

She stopped near him in the doorway, tipped her head to the side, looked at him for a moment and said, "Are we maybe saying I told you so? Are we maybe angling for some line like, 'I'm sorry, Gino, you were absolutely right about me and music teaching'?"

He had to laugh, even while his groin tightened and her scent swam around him. "I think we might be angling for that, yes," he agreed. "But we have your interests in view."

"Who is this *we?*"

"You started it," Gino pointed out.

Hell, he wanted to start something right now. Something physical and simple that didn't require any hard questions or harder answers. He wanted to feel her hair slipping between his fingers, and her skin against his. He wanted to make her cry out in pleasure and cling to him in need. He wanted to laugh with her afterward and do something lazy together, with no pressure, no interruptions and no promises.

"Okay," she conceded. "I started it. Because I'm trying to find a graceful way to say it. You were absolutely right about me and music teaching, Gino. I'm starting to think I might be able to do this. I'm starting to think that the singing was—" She stopped, and scraped her teeth across her lower lip, then looked down. He wanted to reach out and tilt her face back up so that she would have no choice but to look at him.

"Was what?" he asked.

"Was about, oh…" She sighed. "Me trying to fight against all of Harlan's negative messages, or something. But fighting with the wrong weapon. You know, grabbing the wooden spoon instead of the carving knife." She flapped her hands. "I don't know what I'm saying."

"No, I think it makes sense, Roxanna. We don't always fight the right battles in our lives."

She nodded. "That's a better way to put it. There's a reason why Di Bartoli shares keep going up, isn't there? They've got a clever guy in the top job."

The awareness between them crackled in the air like static electricity and notched up another level when he deliberately lowered his voice to say, "That almost sounds like a compliment."

"Ooh, don't get into that kind of wishful thinking, Gino." Her smile teased him.

She tilted her head and folded her arms across her chest, pushing her breasts higher. He thought about how they would press against him if he took her in his arms, thought about how she'd react if he cupped her and ran his thumb over her nipple. A throbbing ache radiated from his core, clamoring to be eased in the only way it could.

In the way it *couldn't,* because she didn't want the only thing he had to offer, and he respected her for that more than he'd imagined possible.

He forced his thoughts onto a different level. "You are going to sing for me one day, before you leave, aren't you?"

"I'm not." She grinned, unfolded her arms and put her hands on her hips.

"Do you realize what a challenge you've set me now? How can I get you to sing if you don't want to? I want to hear your voice, Roxanna."

"Find the right way to ask, I guess." She slipped past him through the doorway.

"And then you will?"

"I'm not promising that there *is* a right way to ask, I should tell you."

"Even more of a challenge, in that case."

"You love a challenge, Gino," she teased him from the safety of the wide front hall.

"You're right. I do."

She didn't give any answer at all to this, just kept smiling as she disappeared up the stairs. He felt more frustrated—sexually and deep in his spirit—than he'd ever been in his life.

So this was the famous Francesco, one-time tormentor of Rox's sister…

He roared up unannounced on Sunday afternoon in an open-topped silver Porsche, leaning on the horn so that any children and livestock who might happen to be in his path would scatter to safety as he wheeled to a halt at the front of the *palazzo*. The combination of horn and engine was aggressive rather than helpful. He took the final turn leaving no margin for error, and his left front headlight finished up less than three inches from Rox's knees.

"Rowena's sister," he said, before he'd even climbed out of the car. He was smoother-looking than Gino. *Better*-looking, many women would have thought.

"Yes, that's me."

"You'll have to excuse me, I feel as if I already know you quite intimately." The car door gave a perfectly engineered slam behind him, while he gave a perfectly engineered grin. "If I get confused and take liberties that I shouldn't…" He kissed her on both cheeks in European fashion, his mouth lingering way too long and leaving a trace of moisture that had Rox's fingers itching to reach for a tissue. "I'm sure this must happen to the two of you all the time."

"Not more than once from the same person," she told

him with unmistakable bite. Her pivot was deliberately clumsy, and her foot landed hard on his toe. "Oops, sorry."

She moved toward the house, feeling a tightness across her face that suggested she might have gotten a sunburn. She'd been outside since eight this morning and had even eaten her lunch on the go. Now it was almost four. She was tired and in no mood for any antics from Gino's younger brother.

Rowie had asked her about the weather on the phone last night and had concluded, "You'll have to hand-water tomorrow, since the drip irrigation system isn't connected yet, and there's no rain in the forecast until midweek. The roses and seedlings you planted and watered on Friday will be fine, but the ones you did earlier last week will need a good soak, and those new stretches of lawn have to be kept damp. You're not forgetting that?"

Rox wasn't, but it had been a long job on her own. She was glad the gardeners would be back tomorrow morning and that the irrigation system would be connected over the next couple of days. On Friday, she was due to leave.

"Wait!" Francesco said. "Aren't you going to keep me company? No-one's come out. Where is everyone?"

Visiting friends of Lisette's on the far side of Siena, but Rox didn't want to admit that she was almost alone here. "Oh, around somewhere," she said vaguely. "Excuse me, Francesco. I'm going up to my room, but I'll tell Maria you're here. Are you staying the night?"

"Is that an invitation?"

"No, since this is your house, not mine. It's a suggestion."

"Suggestions are good, too. I'm very open."

She said patiently, in clarification, "Do please tell

Maria if you're staying, is what I'm suggesting, so that she can make up a room for you and add extra sauce to the chicken."

He laughed. "This is definitely the woman who slammed down the phone a couple of weeks ago, not the woman who couldn't make up her mind how she felt about me."

"Trust me, I know exactly how I feel about you."

"And I like that." He quickened his stride and caught up to her, grabbed her shoulder and pulled her around. His eyes went right to her breasts, then flicked back up. "I know how I feel about you, too. You are your twin, attractive and intelligent but with so much more bite. Don't think I'm angry about our phone conversation. I was, but when I learned the truth about you and your sister…You and I share the same spirit, I think."

"We don't!"

She saw a repetition of the Luigi scenario coming at her like an express train and would actually have preferred Luigi himself. His approach at least had been good-natured and almost cute in its youthful overconfidence. After Rowie's experience, she wasn't prepared to forgive Francesco so easily. Her spine began to crawl the way it did when one of the gardeners accidentally cut an earthworm in two.

Problem was, in this case she couldn't cover Gino's younger brother with a sprinkle of dirt and watch him writhe his way safely under the ground to grow a new back half. She still had to think about the importance of Rowena's résumé and play nice.

"Sorry, Francesco, I'm filthy and hot and I'm taking a shower," she said, edging away.

She heard another car—Gino's—coming toward the house at a much safer speed than Francesco's Porsche had done. He heard it, too, and they both turned. Rox breathed a sigh of relief, while Francesco swore between his teeth.

Thirty seconds later, Pia catapulted into Rox's arms and launched into a verbal replay of their whole day. Gino and Francesco greeted each other with hands slapped hard and hearty on upper arms. Pia's happy flood of words wasn't quite loud enough to drown out Francesco's complaint to his brother, "American women, who can understand them?"

Gino appeared at the door of Roxanna's room about fifteen minutes later, just as she finished getting dressed after her shower. "What did my brother say to you?"

"Uh, come in," she invited him uncertainly.

"No, I'll stay right here. I just want to know what he said."

"What makes you think he said anything?"

"Because I know him, because he's complaining about you, and because of the way you didn't listen to Pia and just disappeared."

"Is she okay? I'm sorry about abandoning her like that, I—"

"Yes, you're sorry because it isn't something you normally do, so I want to know what Francesco said. Or did."

She sighed. "Both." Then she shook her head. "Nothing, really."

"Come on, Roxanna."

"If you know him, then you can guess. He already feels he knows me quite intimately, because of Rowena.

He thinks we share the same spirit. He thinks that slamming the phone down on him two weeks ago is a clear indication that I'll be fabulous in bed." She gave an upside-down smile. "You know, the feisty, clothes-ripping type."

"He said that?"

"He didn't have to."

"No. I suppose he didn't. Look, I apolo—"

"Stop. You don't have to apologize. I can handle him. Far better than my sister could." She smirked. "And I've already practiced recently, on Luigi!"

He smiled, then pressed the pads of his fingers gently to her lips. Her whole body began to tingle and she wanted to melt against him like honey in the sun. "I'm not apologizing for Francesco, Roxanna," he said. "I'm apologizing for me."

"You don't have to do that, either, Gino. It wasn't...the worst idea in the world." *Oh dear lord, no,* her body said. She sighed again. "It just wasn't the right idea for me."

"No, I understand that now."

As if on cue, they both heard Lisette's voice on the stairs. "Gino? Are you up here?"

"Yes, I'm coming down," he called back—to the woman for whom his mistress idea was exactly right, judging from the possessive, sensual way Lisette had touched him a couple of times today.

His eyes met Rox's and they read each other like two open books.

Do you really think I should take what's on offer, Gino's face said.

Well, hey, it'd be your funeral, Rox's expression told him in reply. *But it would be a pretty splashy one.*

* * *

The sound of Roxanna's bedroom door closing between them struck a note of restlessness in Gino's spirits that he didn't understand. His male needs clawed at his body like a swarm of insects, leaving him no peace. Lisette was willing and available, and she understood the rules. So did her husband, who, on his frequent business trips, rarely traveled alone. If two out of the three key players had no problem with the arrangement, then what could be wrong with it?

Many men in Gino's position would sleep with her. Probably tonight.

Because if he didn't tonight, then he'd have to wait until he was back in Rome, which wouldn't be for at least another ten days. At the moment, he didn't feel he could wait ten minutes for physical release.

And yet he couldn't go downstairs to Lisette.

Not now.

Not ever.

Instead, he retreated to his room and attempted to scrape up some control over his mood and his body.

Cold water was the traditional method. He stripped and took an icy shower, then dropped to the floor with his towel still wrapped around his waist and did twenty push-ups. They did nothing for him, and he growled aloud through gritted teeth at his own helpless, painful state all the way through getting dressed.

He must sound like an animal! He felt like one…

And he'd told Lisette that he was coming down about twenty minutes ago. What would she think about the fact that he hadn't appeared?

As he loped down the stairs, her voice was the first

thing he heard, but he almost didn't recognize it. She was yelling. The sound came from the *salone,* so he went in that direction and heard a whiplike crack just as he came through the open double doors.

One look at the red mark on Pia's cheek as she sat at the piano told Gino what had made that ugly sound— the flat of Lisette's hand coming hard across his daughter's face.

He was so shocked that he froze in place.

Lisette looked like a hare caught in a spotlight. Her eyes glittered with anger, but she went on the defensive at once. "She said she was 'practicing,' Gino, but honestly it was just noise—loud, loud noise; I have a splitting headache, and she didn't stop when I asked."

"And you hit her." Pia had certainly stopped playing now.

"A child has to have discipline."

"Across the face. The sound of it *echoed.*"

"A little harder than I meant to." She turned to Pia and bent over her. "Sweetheart, Aunt Lisette lost her temper. Can I kiss you better?"

Pia flinched but didn't move, still too shocked, and Lisette interpreted this as a yes. She kissed the little red cheek. Gino could see his daughter struggling not to cry. No, struggling to breathe. Her shoulders heaved as she took in several brittle, ineffective gasps. He lunged toward her and took her up in his arms. Her chest was as tight as a drum.

"Go back to Rome, Lisette," he said over the top of Pia's head.

"I'm sorry. I lost my temper."

"You're not a house-bound, overworked, twenty-year-old nanny or an impoverished single parent left alone with a squabbling brood for fifteen hours a day. Losing your temper is not an excuse. Your headache is not an excuse. Not when we have all been trying so hard with Pia for so many months. Not when Roxanna has done more for her in two and a half weeks than Meess Cassidi did in four years. Cry, darling," he told his daughter. "Let yourself cry."

It was the only way she'd start to breathe properly.

He felt the long, drawn-out shudder of her in-breath and steeled himself for the deafening pitch of her screams that soon came. For the first time in Pia's life, he felt relieved at the sound and acted purely on instinct, swaying rhythmically on his feet and making quiet shushing sounds, content to be patient until she calmed herself down in her own way and in her own time.

His love for his little daughter swept over him like a fresh ocean tide and it was the best feeling he'd ever had. *Could I have gotten to this point without Roxanna?* he wondered. *I can't let her fly home without knowing how grateful I am.*

"Go back to Rome, Gino?" Lisette asked, her voice timid and her smile tentative. "You mean that?"

"Yes. We don't need each other. Not in the way you suggested yesterday at lunch. I didn't seriously consider it for a moment, and I should have told you so at once. You're Angele's sister and Pia's aunt, but nothing more, and right now…" He shook his head, not wanting to create a rift he might later regret. "Just take Nicoletta and go back to Rome."

She bit her lip. "I really am sorry. I'm not a patient person. I—I was wrong, and I'm sorry."

"I know you're sorry," Gino said. "But still I want you to go back to Rome."

"I thought Lisette and Nicoletta were staying until tomorrow morning," Francesco said over the evening meal.

Maria's chicken cacciatore was fabulous, as usual, but Gino's appetite had fallen flat and he knew she'd be disappointed in him. Pia, in contrast, had sat beautifully at the big dining table and eaten like a horse, only with much better table manners.

"Is this anything to do with the raised voices and the tantrum from little missy that I heard coming from the *salone* earlier?" Francesco asked.

"It wasn't a tantrum," Gino answered.

"The screaming, then."

"We'll talk about this later, Francesco."

"You were angry with Lisette, I know that."

"You're not going to let it go, are you?" Gino saw Roxanna's instinctive glance in his direction. She looked uncomfortable, but she said nothing.

"Okay, okay, I'll let it go. Maria, is there dessert?" Francesco asked the housekeeper as she came back into the dining room.

"There's my *panforte* with coffee in the *salone* whenever you want it."

"Come, Pia, your Uncle Francesco is taking you to play while my stomach makes room for more of Maria's cooking," Francesco announced. When he could be bothered, he was very good with children. Gino hoped that he would be bothered more often, once he and Marcellina were married and had children of their own.

"That might take a while, because I've already eaten waaay too much…"

"Piggyback ride, Uncle 'ncesco?"

"Hey, you know they're my number-one specialty, princess." Francesco threw his niece up in the air and swung her deftly around to sit high on his shoulders. "Duck your head under the door!"

They disappeared, and Maria did, too.

A silence fell.

He and Roxanna were good at those, Gino decided.

Possibly it was their number-one specialty.

Before she could think up either an escape plan or a conversation topic, he said, "Tell me what happened on Saturday morning when Pia cut up the dress. What happened before I came in and found the three of you in my office."

Her shoulders tensed. "Well, Lisette wanted Pia to stop cutting, and Pia fought her on it."

"But what did Lisette say? The same things she said this afternoon? In the same voice?"

Roxanna didn't answer for a moment, then she said quickly, "She didn't hit her, Gino."

"You heard today?"

"I was coming down the stairs. Too late to hear, but I saw Pia's face over your shoulder with the red mark on one cheek, and I guessed."

"And you weren't surprised."

"No."

"You beat a strategic retreat?"

"Uh, yes, I didn't think it was my, um, role to get in the way."

"But Lisette yelled at Pia the other day?"

Roxanna just looked at him.

"So you knew? And you said nothing to me?"

"I'm only your surrogate garden contractor, Gino."

"You're Pia's—" He stopped. There wasn't a word for what Roxanna was to Pia—or to him—and the gap in his vocabulary felt too wide and too deep and just *wrong*.

"I'm her friend," Roxanna said. "But Lisette's her aunt. And your…well…lover, I assume. Soon-to-be lover. That's your business," she added hastily. "I wanted to say something. I would have done if she'd hit Pia, because that's clear-cut. But just to report words and tone…" She shook her head. "If you hadn't wanted to believe me, trying to tell you might only have made everything worse."

Gino nodded, recognizing the truth in what she said. He couldn't blame her for remaining silent.

"Excuse me, I think I'll skip dessert tonight," she said. "I have to call Rowena with a couple of questions about the work in the garden this week, and it should be a good time to catch her at home. If I don't come down again tonight…"

"Your time is your own, Roxanna," Gino told her. "You don't have to account for it to me."

She spread her hands and looked helpless. "I know, but…"

They looked at each other, and the air crackled. She stood up slowly, and there was a point where Gino thought she would come around the table and touch him, and give him the cue—or the excuse—that he needed to take her in his arms and slake his desire in a way he never could have done with Lisette, even if he'd jumped at what she was offering.

But Roxanna didn't come to him. She headed for the door instead. As Gino watched her depart—back and shoulders and graceful walk—she seemed more vulnerable than usual, and half the warmth in the room seemed to get sucked out of it as soon as she'd gone.

Chapter Ten

"Rox, you have been so great about this," Rowena said on the phone on Thursday night, after they'd discussed the final list of instructions that Rox would give the gardeners tomorrow morning before she left. "I've disrupted your life, your career…"

"No, Rowie."

"Yes! You don't have to shield me like that! Your industry magazines are getting forwarded in the mail from New Jersey, and I've seen the auditions you're missing out on."

"It's not a problem. Seriously, it's not."

How could she explain everything to Rowena in a long-distance call? Her thinking had changed and cleared, and she saw her professional future so differently now. They'd have to talk about it back home. She was ticketed direct to Newark, New Jersey, but she planned to fly down to Florida sometime over the next couple of weeks to see her family.

By then, it should all seem even clearer, and with some time and distance, she would maybe manage to leave Gino out of the picture, too. She would definitely leave him out, because she had to. He'd made it clear that they didn't belong in each other's lives.

When she and Rowena had finished their call, she went over to the window seat that she'd grown to love and looked out over the moonlit rows of vines beyond the newly unfolding garden.

How do I feel about singing now? It's still important...

But more private. For herself, not for an audience. For her own creative release, not to prove a point to a man she'd once been married to but didn't need to obsess over anymore.

She cleared her throat, produced an experimental hum.

Hi, singing voice. How're you feeling today?

Mmm, not bad.

She sang a scale, her pitch clear and true, then launched into the first two lines of a bitter and cynical song she'd written during the divorce.

Nope. That's not how I'm feeling tonight.

Through the window, the full moon seemed to be listening, watching over Pia as she drifted to sleep, watching over Rox with its eternally wise, sad face. Without even reaching a conscious decision about it, she discovered herself starting on "Moon River," a little scratchy at first, then mellow and low and strong.

It was such a poignant, whimsical song. A woman like Rox could read her whole life into Johnny Mercer's lyrics if she wanted to.

She didn't hear the door open, but a few minutes later when she'd finished the song, she heard Gino's applause. She gasped as she turned away from the window and saw him.

"I'm sorry for sneaking in," he said at once. "But I could hear you on my way past after kissing Pia good-night. It was beautiful, and I knew you'd stop if you heard me."

She couldn't help smiling. "Beautiful? Really? Thanks." It meant so much to her, coming from Gino.

"You're very good." He moved farther into the room and she came to meet him, stopping beside the antique cedar chest that sat at the foot of the bed.

"But I'm not great," she said, looking up at him.

"There are plenty of singers out there who make a decent living in hotel lounge bars even when they're not great."

"Except that it's not what I want. I'm the all-or-nothing type. Haven't we talked about that?"

"We have. And I can't imagine you any different."

"You've given me something very important while I've been here, Gino—the idea that I could teach, and be good at it and enjoy it. It's going to be better for me than singing, where I'd only ever be going after that rainbow's end that Johnny Mercer talked about and watching it recede with every step I took."

"The giving has gone both ways, Roxanna."

"Has it?" She felt insanely happy that he thought so. *I'm leaving something valuable here. Something for Gino.*

"You've given me my daughter."

"Oh, Gino, you've always had your daughter! She loves you."

"But I never knew who she was. She was always my Difficult Child, now she's Pia. She's unique. Bright and creative and full of life. Impatient and unforgiving, too, sometimes. But she's not a problem to be dealt with and handled and solved." His eyes seemed to darken. "If I have a problem right now, Roxanna, it's you."

"Me?" she echoed stupidly.

"You know…You know what I'm talking about." He lifted her arm and kissed the soft inner skin at her elbow. Rox closed her eyes and felt the warm press of his mouth against her neck. "You know," he said again. His voice was only a whisper, and his kisses touched her jaw, her cheek, the corner of her mouth.

She couldn't speak. His face was so warm and right against hers, the press of his cheek, the scent of his skin.

"I want you so much. One night, Roxanna. Give me that. And take it away with you, also. The memory of one night together. Don't think any farther ahead than that. Couldn't we give each other one night?"

"No…" But she began to kiss him anyhow. She couldn't help it, knew how dangerous it was, couldn't think of stopping.

His arms wrapped around her, and she felt him trembling with need. Their kiss deepened until her mouth felt swollen and tingling and numb, and the rest of her body sang. He found her breasts beneath her tank top and sweater, and she wished there were no clothing to get in their way. She wanted to run her hands over his chest, kiss a trail of fire down his belly, discover every inch of him.

"You said no," he whispered.

She couldn't answer. It just came out as a moan of need and uncertainty from deep in her throat.

I said no, but I want this so much. Do I care about tomorrow? Will tomorrow change if I say yes?

Her body tensed, and he felt it. He pulled away, far enough to see her face. Looking into his eyes, she traced the gorgeous shape of his mouth with acutely sensitized fingertips, then laid her palm against his jaw. He covered it with his own hand. "This isn't what you want, is it?" he said. "It has never been what you wanted."

"Oh, it's what I want. My whole body wants it. But it's, oh, not what I *need*. And *need* is the word I have to listen to."

His breath rasped between his teeth. "Do you know how hard this is for me?"

"Yes. I do. Because it's no easier for me. Trust me on that, Gino!" She let out a jerky laugh.

"All right, that was unfair. I can't blackmail you, can I?" He pivoted away from her, his energy turning inward as he struggled to gain control.

"You probably could," she admitted. "I think you could do pretty much anything you wanted with me right now."

She closed her eyes and waited, having no idea what he'd do with the power she'd just given him with those last words.

"Nice try, Roxanna," he said several seconds later, his voice coming from near the door. "But I'm not going to have you hating me by the time you leave tomorrow."

He'd slipped out into the corridor before she had time to decide how to reply.

* * *

Checklist time.

The computerized irrigation system had been connected on Wednesday and tested in all its glory in the midst of nine hours of steady, pouring rain. In Florida, Rowena had finalized the text for each plaque, had it professionally translated and gotten estimates from several ceramic companies on the cost of creating the plaques out of clay. New paving stones had been delivered and partially laid yesterday, and the freshly planted stretches of grass showed velvety green against the earth.

The roses had started to unfold their spring growth, first in little knobs of red and green pushing out from the dormant canes, then in pleated fans of tender, shiny leaves that were almost purple in hue. The miraculous beauty of it entranced Rox, but couldn't distract her from the fact that she was leaving today and would probably never see Gino Di Bartoli or his daughter again.

They couldn't have become so important to her in such a short time. She kept telling herself this, but her heart didn't listen. She'd packed her things already, and Gino and Pia were driving her to the airport in half an hour. The sun had come out from behind the clouds today, but she felt as if it might not even rise tomorrow in New Jersey.

"I didn't even *like* him that first day," she scolded herself as she walked back to the house after her final consultation with the gardeners. The memory didn't help. A tear broke loose from her lashes and trickled down her cheek. She wiped it away with the heel of her hand, no doubt leaving a muddy mark.

She'd just said goodbye to Benno, Salvatore and Luigi, that was why she was crying.

Ug, no it wasn't. Saying goodbye to the gardeners had been only a rehearsal for saying goodbye to Gino and Pia.

She'd let all three of the men give her a hearty kiss on each cheek, and when Luigi had offered marriage—"I'm a good hard worker"—she'd asked the other two, "What do you think, guys? Should I accept? The age difference is a bit of a concern."

"Exactly!" Benno had told her. "You don't want a man who's just starting out, you want one who already has money in the bank."

I want Gino.

And I'd take him penniless.

Right now, I'd take him for ninety seconds in the back of a delivery truck, next to someone else's trees.

She could have had him in much greater comfort than that on Sunday night, but he'd understood enough…had strength enough…to make the decision for both of them and leave her dangerous bedroom before the explosion took place.

Still, over the past four days, their tension and need had lingered in the air, like the smell of cordite after fireworks, even though the fireworks had never happened. It was good that they'd both been busy. Gino had shut himself away in his office with Francesco for most of Monday, while Pia played at her friend Ciara's house. On Tuesday, he'd made a quick business trip to Florence.

Today, there would be no chance of avoiding each other until after they'd said their final goodbye. They'd be shut away together in the front of his car, with Pia in the back, all the way from here to the airport. After they'd delivered her to her flight, Pia and Gino were spending some time in Rome.

When she reached the house, her bags were already waiting in the front hall, along with the remaining suitcase of Rowie's that she'd packed. Pia sat at the kitchen table drinking some juice, and Maria told Rox, "Signor Gino is bringing the car from the garage."

Rox hated goodbyes.

She could never get them right.

When you were the all-or-nothing type, goodbyes were hard.

She and Maria hugged and wished each other all good things, then hugged again and almost cried, but they'd only known each other for just over three weeks, so…

I can't act as if this is the end of the world, even though that's exactly how it feels.

How much worse would it be with Pia and Gino?

Much.

Much worse.

Rox held it together during the car journey. She held it together when Gino dropped her in front of the terminal with her baggage and went with Pia to park his car. She held it together while Gino and Pia stood near her at the check-in desk and on her way to the bathroom on her own.

But when she came out of the bathroom and saw Gino and Pia amongst the crowds of people, just the way she'd first seen them at this same airport three weeks and two days ago, she lost it. And when you were the all-or-nothing type, you really couldn't hide your tears.

"I need the bathroom, Papa," Pia told Gino while they waited endlessly for Roxanna's return. Why was she taking so long?

We should have said goodbye at the check-in desk, he thought. There was no reason to prolong it like this.

But if they'd said goodbye at the check-in desk, then it would be over, and that thought seemed unbearable. Waiting for her to come back from the bathroom was bad enough. How the hell would he ever say goodbye?

Gino took Pia by the hand, led her in the right direction and told her just outside the bathroom door, "I'll wait for you right here, okay? Call for Roxanna…Maddie. She must still be in here, I think."

He waited some more.

No Roxanna.

He heard Pia's voice calling out, and then she appeared. "She's not in there, Papa."

"No?" he murmured and started looking around. "Are you sure?"

"I called, and she didn't answer, and then I said it's not a game anymore, and when you say that, then the hiding person has to come out, but she didn't. Papa, I think she's lost."

Lost? Like Pia herself, three weeks ago?

No, Gino realized, *I'm the one who's lost.*

He would be utterly lost if he let her go.

Rox hid behind a column with a travel poster on it and sobbed.

"This is insane, Roxanna Madison," she hissed to herself. "You can't cry until after you've said goodbye. Just stop. Or he'll know. Oh damn, my eyes must be swollen half out of my head. Just get a grip and get back to the bathroom so you can wash your face."

Then she heard Pia's voice, getting closer with every

word. "Maddie, are you lost? Maddie, we're not playing hide-and-seek. It's not a game, so you have to come out. Maddie? I'm soon going to get most concerned!" *Darling little thing, she still channeled Queen Victoria occasionally.*

And I'm not going to hear her doing it anymore…

Rox stepped out from behind the safe refuge of the column and bent down, not even sure how she'd managed to make the move. "I'm here, sweetheart." Her voice rasped, as thin as tissue paper. "It's okay."

"I thought you were lost." Pia saw Rox's red, tear-sodden face. "You *were* lost! You were crying!"

Rox managed a smile. "Know what? I'm still lost, sweetheart," she whispered. "That's why I'm crying. Lost in Italy…my heart is…with you and your papa…and I don't think I'll ever get it back to bring it home."

But Pia was only four. She didn't understand—fortunately. "You're not lost anymore, silly! Papa and I have found you now, so it's okay."

Papa…?

Rox looked up to find him crossing the last piece of polished terminal floor between them.

Oh damn, she thought again.

Had he heard? Were her eyes still such a betraying red?

He didn't give her the time or space to work it out. "I've been so stupid," he said. His arms came around her. "I can't let you go. Stay, Roxanna, and be a part of my life, and Pia's."

"A *part* of it, Gino?" she whispered. "How can I do that? What is there here for me? We've talked about this! What would you do? Set me up in an apartment in Rome, so I could wait for you every evening? Maybe get lucky a couple of times a week, in between your work and Pia? Wait for a great big ax to fall someday, when you were ready to move on? What would I be left with then?"

"No!" He swore. "No, I don't mean it like that! Not anymore. You've done something to me, Roxanna. I've discovered I'm the all-or-nothing type, too, and the thought of nothing is simply unbearable. When it comes to you, I want it all. I want all of you. I love you…"

"So do I," said a little voice nearby. Rox felt the fabric of her trousers tighten around her thigh as Pia clung to it.

"…and if I'd had any sense," Gino said, "I would have understood my own heart a little sooner—last night, or on Sunday—and not left something as momentous and important and *necessary* as a marriage proposal until the last minute like this." He muttered something under his breath and buried his face in the curve of her neck. "What can I do? Your flight leaves in an hour!"

"I don't have to be on it," Rox said. She'd always been comfortable with leaving important things until the last minute.

He pulled back and looked at her. "Are you saying yes?"

She looked back at him, her gaze every bit as intense. "Are you really asking, Gino? You said you never would."

"Because I thought that if I couldn't make it work with someone perfect like Angele, then I couldn't make it work with anyone. But then I discovered that I didn't want perfection, I wanted you."

"Me, with all my imperfections? That's the nicest thing anyone's ever said…Oh, Gino!"

"You," he whispered. "Intuitive and emotional and alive. The all-or-nothing type."

"Who doesn't know when to let a subject go?"

"And isn't afraid to share her opinions. Life is much more interesting that way."

"Takes off her garden gloves and gets her hands way too dirty?"

"I love that. And I love how much you care about your sister, and the bond you have with Pia." His arms went tight and hard around her again. "Roxanna, you have to tell me, are you really brave enough to say yes to a man who told you just a few weeks ago that he'd never ask?"

"Yes." Harlan's Reasons Number Thirteen and Nineteen, which added up to a kind of bravery, it turned out. She was always changing her plans, and she didn't know what was good for her.

Only he was wrong, because this time I do.

"Yes?" He pressed his forehead against hers, tilted his head and kissed her.

"Absolutely one hundred percent yes, Gino." She curved her palm softly over his jaw. "We should go back to the check-in desk and tell them we need to get my bags off the flight."

"Shall we explain to Pia?" Gino said. "Or wait until we've worked out when—"

"Get Maddie's bags off!" Pia let go of Rox's trouser leg and darted between a cluster of businessmen. She disappeared in seconds, but they could still hear her eager little voice. "Maddie is staying. We have to get her bags off! Does that mean we get to go on the moving thing ourselves?"

"I think she's way ahead of us," Rox said. "She has all the important stuff worked out already."

"We'll lose her if we're not careful."

"Then let's catch up." She took his arm and they apologized as they made their way through the milling people.

"Roxanna?"

"Yes, Gino?"

"I think we have all the important stuff worked out already, too."

Rox had no desire to argue. Agreeing with a husband could get to be a very nice habit, she decided. But only when that husband was Gino.

* * * * *

SILHOUETTE *Romance*®

COMING NEXT MONTH

#1818 CHASING DREAMS—Cara Colter

Book-smart and reserved, Jessica King instinctively knows she needs someone to bring her inner wild child out. And though she's engaged to a somewhat stuffy academic, something tells her that earthy mechanic Garner Blake, whom she has just met, may be more the man of her dreams…. But can she find the courage now to listen to her heart and not her head?

#1819 WISHING AND HOPING—Susan Meier

Word on the street is that Tia Capriotti is suddenly marrying Drew Wallace, a longtime neighbor *and* her father's best friend. But inquiring minds want to know—is there something political afoot in their courtship? And what is that subtle bulge at her belly?

#1820 IF THE SLIPPER FITS—Elizabeth Harbison

Concierge; browbeaten orphan—they might be one and the same, with the way Prince Conrad's stepmother treats hostess Lily Tilden in her own boutique hotel. To uncover the jewel that is hers and Conrad's love, Lily must first overcome the royal tricks of this woman, who seems to have studied carefully the wicked women of yore!

#1821 THE PARENT TRAP—Lissa Manley

Divorcée Jill Lindstrom and widower Brandon Clark each just wanted to leave hectic lives and open landmark restaurants in the small Oregon town. But their cooking mixtures seem bland when compared to the elaborate schemes their daughters concoct to give the pair a taste of how delicious their lives could be together….